Interstate Motorcycles

written by Laurel
Janis cousins
husband

3/2012

BILL DUNKUS

Interstate Motorcycles
A DEALER'S TALE

iUniverse, Inc.
Bloomington

Interstate Motorcycles
A Dealer's Tale

Copyright © 2011 by Bill Dunkus.

All rights reserved. No part of this book may be used or reproduced by any means, graphic, electronic, or mechanical, including photocopying, recording, taping or by any information storage retrieval system without the written permission of the publisher except in the case of brief quotations embodied in critical articles and reviews.

This is a work of fiction. All of the characters, names, incidents, organizations, and dialogue in this novel are either the products of the author's imagination or are used fictitiously. iUniverse books may be ordered through booksellers or by contacting:

iUniverse
1663 Liberty Drive
Bloomington, IN 47403
www.iuniverse.com
1-800-Authors (1-800-288-4677)

Because of the dynamic nature of the Internet, any web addresses or links contained in this book may have changed since publication and may no longer be valid. The views expressed in this work are solely those of the author and do not necessarily reflect the views of the publisher, and the publisher hereby disclaims any responsibility for them.

Any people depicted in stock imagery provided by Thinkstock are models, and such images are being used for illustrative purposes only.
Certain stock imagery © Thinkstock.

ISBN: 978-1-4620-5649-1 (sc)
ISBN: 978-1-4620-5651-4 (hc)
ISBN: 978-1-4620-5650-7 (ebk)

Printed in the United States of America

iUniverse rev. date: 09/30/2011

BASED ON ACTUAL EVENTS.

PROLOGUE

IT IS ALWAYS REMARKABLE to me when a man tells me he doesn't have a motorcycle only because his wife will not let him have one. What a crock. I would have a lot more respect for those individuals if they would just say they don't want one, or can't afford one, or even if they would just honestly say that they are fearful of the darn things. Blaming their wives for not having one, however, is a cheap shot at their wives, who are probably lovely people. When I hear men say it, which is incredibly often, I never really believe it. By the way, it comes up often because I am a motorcycle dealer. My wife, Lori, and I are partners in a small motorcycle dealership in rural Missouri, and my primary income-producing function is to work the sales floor, although I do all of the other functions at the shop as the workload and staffing levels require. Lori and I have enjoyed motorcycling together, as both a wonderful hobby and as a business that has provided a decent living for us. An old friend and business associate once told me that motorcycles have been good to me. He was right. That is, until Wall Street crashed and burned the financial markets, the US auto industry self-destructed, banks began to fail in numbers only slightly rivaled by the Great Depression, and unemployment rose to the double-digit percentages. All of which stopped motorcycle sales in 2008 and 2009 as solidly as Noah's ark must have been when it finally ran aground. You want an honest reason for not buying a motorcycle? How about "I don't know how I'm going to pay the rent, much less buy a motorcycle"? I can't argue with that, and I'm hearing it a lot lately.

We have finished the last six business quarters in the red. We have had to beg our bankers to continue to loan us money just to make expenses, much of which includes interest payments on previously borrowed money. All of this is an attempt to keep our little enterprise afloat until economic conditions generally improve. In fact the downturn in income has led me to choices that are far more hazardous than just hefty interest. While just trying to keep things together, I've crossed over into dangerous territory and deadly decisions. All I really want is for folks to get back to work and for banks to start lending money so our customers can buy bikes from us again. Then we can get caught back up and back to business as it should be.

Having lived in the Midwest near the Mississippi River my entire life, there have been a number of occasions that I have joined volunteer sandbag teams to stack temporary levies around my neighbors' property to hold back slowly rising floodwaters. The bags have to be stacked higher and wider in a bruising, slow race to stay ahead of the flood crest. It's horrible to watch a disaster happen in slow motion as the Great River gradually claims ground. With a little luck, a lot of sweat, and the will of God, the sandbag levy holds until the water starts to recede and relieve the pressure. Then the massive mess can be cleaned up and everyone gets on with his or her life. That's our current business strategy. I know it's not very encouraging, but it's about all the hope we have for right now. I'm holding out hope that we can survive to the cleanup phase.

By the way, my name is Mike Douglas and our store is called Interstate Motorcycles. We sell new and used bikes, parts, and accessories as well as perform service on most major makes and models of motorcycles and all-terrain vehicles. That's the sales pitch. Here's the story.

DECEMBER 1, 2009

ANOTHER LONG, SLEEPLESS NIGHT. I toss and turn, looking at the red digital display on the alarm clock every minute or two. It's still reading 1:09 a.m. It seems like it has been an hour ago that it was reading 1:02. The more I look at the clock, the slower it seems to move. My brain is buzzing. Anxiety about sales for the year that are way down, again, and the pressure of the end of the year, which is just thirty-one days away, combine to whirl my thoughts. Even though I'm physically and mentally tired, I can't stop thinking about what I can do, or should do, to generate some year-end sales. But that's what comes along with being the boss, and I really wouldn't want it any other way. I knew from the time I was a little boy I wanted to make my living on my own, in business for myself. If the company needs some new ideas and direction, it's ultimately up to me to provide them. It can be a heavy burden. That is probably why Hugh Petrowski yelled a lot. Thinking about him makes me smile. I must have been ten, maybe twelve years old. My dad worked the graveyard shift. When I was at school, he was at home awake. When I got home from school, he was asleep. When I was going to bed at night, he was getting up so he could go to work. Our schedules always kept us away from each other.

I didn't mind, though, because I always knew my dad was an important man. It was the early 1960s. I remember because I was still wearing the "JFK All the Way" campaign button Dad had pinned on me. He was a big John Kennedy supporter because he said Kennedy was for the working man—men like Dad. He was a milkman back in the days when people got their milk delivered straight from the dairy right to their back porch. Milk came in glass bottles and was thick and creamy with a small paper cap on the top. If you were lucky enough to be the first to open the bottle, you could lick the cream off the bottom of the paper cap. It was like a spoonful of ice cream with whipped cream on it. I can still taste it after all these years.

But my dad was not just a milkman; he was the milkman to the milkmen. He worked the graveyard shift, loading the milk trucks for the milkmen who would go out daily and make their rounds, delivering milk to housewives' back porches. If my dad liked a driver, he could make sure the guy had a little extra milk or cream on his truck. The delivery guys could then use the extra product to entice the housewives into extra sales, or favors perhaps. I was an adult before I figured out what Dad and his milkman friends meant when they would kid each other about the kids in the neighborhood looking like the milkmen who delivered to their houses. I didn't mind not being able to see him that much. I always knew he was an important man, and I always knew Saturday was coming. Saturdays were different. Saturdays were our day. I would get up early, even though I didn't have to go to school, and I would wait for him in the backyard. When he got off work in the morning, he would come in through the backyard so he could check our milk cooler on the porch and make sure our delivery was correct. Then he would take the morning's milk into the house, kiss my mom, and give me the wink I couldn't wait to get. The wink

Interstate Motorcycles

meant it was time for us, just me and Dad. I would run out to the car, a 1954 Chevy four-door with single-barrel, side-draft Weber carb on a GM cast-iron, six-cylinder driven through the massive manual transmission with three on the tree. The steering wheel seemed nearly as big in diameter as the car's whitewall tires, with a beautiful chrome-plated horn ring inside that activated the loud, dual-tone horns under the heavy all-American steel hood. He jumped in behind the wheel and I jumped up on his lap. He operated the gas, clutch, and brake and shifted the gears, and I swung that big old steering wheel around like the captain of a steamship heading out to sea. Our first stop was always the Texaco station at the end of the block, where Dad would assist me in steering the car up close to the gas pumps. The rubber hose on the ground that stretched out from the building to the gas pump island sounded the big bell in the garage as our tires rolled over it, and out would pop Moony. He was at the car before we could get out, and Dad would give him the standard order: "A buck's worth of regular."

Moony was a black man whose job was to gas up and service cars at the pumps. I always stayed outside with Moony and talked with him as he busily gassed up and serviced our car. He washed the glass, checked the oil, opened the battery to check its fluid level, and whopped all of the tires with a wooden axe handle to make sure they sounded properly aired. I liked Moony. He always told me jokes and treated me like an adult while he was servicing Dad's car. Dad always went straight back to the garage to say hello to the station's chief mechanic and owner, Hugh Petrowski. I was a little afraid of Mr. Petrowski. He was always greasy and yelled a lot. Both he and my dad made it clear that the garage was off limits to kids like me. There was too much equipment and too many ways for a little guy to get hurt. So once Moony was finished with our car, I would stand outside the garage at the door and wait for Dad. The wooden sign nailed over the top of the door, which was always propped open with a tire, read, "Hugh Petrowski, Entrepreneur."

I didn't know what *entrepreneur* meant, but I knew it was something important because my dad was important and he respected Hugh Petrowski.

It seems like just a minute ago, but I check the alarm clock again. "Six thirty?" I whisper so not to wake up Lori sleeping beside me. *That can't be right.* Rubbing my eyes and angling the thing to get a better look, I see that it actually is 6:30 a.m. "Crap." Normally I'm up at 5:00, and this morning especially I needed to be up on time. I have a long task list to do *first thing.*

I reach to Lori's side of the bed and feel that it is empty. She is already up. Stumbling into the bathroom, I find her already in the shower. "I overslept. Why didn't you wake me?"

"You tossed and turned most of the night. When you finally did get to sleep, I thought you'd better sleep for a while," she says as she turns off the water and pulls her towel in.

"I probably kept you up. I'm sorry. Once I finally did get to sleep, it seems that I was only asleep for a minute."

"You didn't keep me up. I slept pretty good."

As she exits the shower, I drop off my shorts and enter. After quickly washing, I shave fast enough to cause two nicks, brush the teeth, get dressed, and meet her again by the coffeemaker. "I've got to go," I tell her as I shoot down a half cup of coffee.

"Mike," she says, sounding like my mother, "you can't go to work looking like that."

"What?"

"Look at those jeans! They're full of holes."

Interstate Motorcycles

"They are the only clean ones I have."

"And where did you get that sweatshirt? You could fit two of you in there."

"I will change into a work shirt at the shop, as always. What difference does it make?"

"You have a fit build for a fifty-five-year-old guy. I just think you should let it show a little better."

"I'm saving it all for you, baby. Besides I just look like an old guy anymore with all this gray hair."

"Just the right amount of gray," she says, stroking the hair at my temples. "You look distinguished."

"I have to go," I tell her again as I hug her.

"I'll get there as quick as I can," she answers as I plant a quick kiss on her.

Now I am really in a hurry. At 7:15 a.m. I roll the bike out of the garage, start it, and let it warm up while I get my jacket, helmet, and gloves on and do a quick walk-around pre-ride inspection. *Is that rear tire low?* I grab the tire gauge for a checkup. The rear tire on the Moto Guzzi 1100 Breva is easy to get at so I don't have to pull off my gear.

It wasn't low yesterday so I must have picked up something to cause a leak on the way home last night. *Well, that's going to cause a change in plans.* I was going to make a loop through town and hit the bank, post office, our insurance agent's office to drop off a payment, and then the grocery for some lunch meat before I go to work and open the store by nine o'clock.

Now what I should do is drop the bike by the shop and make the rounds in our service truck. *I'll never get it all in!*

Don't you hate it when you haven't even left the house and your day is already running behind schedule? I form an alternate plan. As I air the tire back up to operating pressure with the emergency pump in the garage, I figure I'll dump the post office and grocery stops on Lori, hustle to the bank and make a fast deposit to cover the insurance payment, which will be late if not dropped off first thing this morning. Then I can hit the insurance company, drop off the check, and make tracks to the shop to get open before this tire goes low and causes me any more trouble. *That should work. It seems to be a slow leak.* So I'm hoping anyway.

"Lori!" I bellow as I fight the little air chuck onto the rear tire's valve stem. "Oh, Lori!"

"What?" she shouts back as she opens the door between our kitchen and the garage.

"I need you to go by the post office and Country Mart before you go to work."

"No way, I have to stop by the church to write some checks." She's the church treasurer. "I'm going to be there late as it is."

"That's all right," I answer as I pull back away from the tire and look up the stairs at her. I have to pause for just a second and admire her. She is the prettiest woman I've ever known: gorgeous blonde hair and ever-smiling Irish green eyes. "Look, I've got a flat tire and I've got to make this deposit the moment the bank opens and drop off this insurance payment before they cancel us."

Interstate Motorcycles

"Well, okay, but I'm going to be late and I don't want you giving me that look when I get there. I haven't even fixed my hair yet. It's a mess."

"No, it's not, and I won't give you that look. You have to do it. These checks have to get in the mail today or they will be late too. It's the first of the month."

"It is a mess," she says as she sighs. "I better get moving." And off she goes fluffing her damp hair with both hands.

That being handled, I mounted the bike and tear off down the drive toward the highway and the bank. I figure if the tire is leaking slowly, the smart money is to make the run quickly and get it parked in our service department to be checked out later, before it gets low again. It is December and, although rather pleasant for this time of year, at forty-five degrees the weather can be rather brisk. But it's dry and above freezing so traction shouldn't be compromised. Actually, bundled up as I was and with the handgrip heaters on, I was quite comfortable. Zipping along on the twisty two-lane highway toward town, I was happily recalling how much I still enjoy riding motorcycles, even after all these years. There was no other traffic so I could relax a bit and let my mind fast-forward to today's other tasks at work. I knew I had some bikes we had serviced getting picked up, one of which was going to be uncomfortable. Gene Stanford had brought it to us for an oil change and minor tune-up and we had found the bike actually needed an engine overhaul. When we contacted the customer with our findings, he became indignant, thinking we were trying to up-sell him to a big job he was sure he didn't need, or want. We of course ended the job right there and suggested he pick up the bike, pay us for the service we had performed, checking it out, and take it elsewhere for a second opinion. All of which he agreed to except paying for what we had already completed. He wasn't willing to pay anything that would have amounted to a thorough diagnostic performed for him at my expense. We are going to have to negotiate something, and I'm sure it won't be easy with this guy.

One of my favorite turns is at hand: a sweeping lefthander that you can bank the bike into and roll up the throttle. I swerve the bike left and right several times as I approach and feel out that rear tire. Feels normal, indicating it is holding pressure, so I set up wide right for the turn and slide my hips slightly off the saddle toward the left. I enter the turn fast, get on the line, and roll up a handful of throttle, accelerating through. Beautiful!

Following this pleasant distraction, my thoughts rewind back to how I will handle Mr. Stanford. Then the high-pitched shriek of an emergency vehicle siren interrupts my thoughts. I check my instruments to see my speed and read eighty-five miles per hour. Without flinching, I go hard to the brakes and begin scanning my mirrors in hope that it is an ambulance behind me. No such luck. A highway patrol car is in hot pursuit and this day's problems, which I already thought might be tough enough, are about to get much tougher. I immediately pull over.

"Going a little fast back there, aren't you, sir?" the remarkably young-looking, tall and lean trooper says as he moves toward me while adjusting his Smokey the Bear hat. The officer's appearance is both impeccable and menacing. With a sharp, creased blouse and trousers and spit-shined leather and brass, he eyes me and the European sport bike with a high degree of contempt. Since I have said nothing in response to his first question, he poses for me another, this time with even more authority in his tone. "Do you know how fast you were going back there, sir?"

If you have ever found yourself in this situation, you already know there is no good answer to that question. As I pause to

Interstate Motorcycles

collect my thoughts, so does he. This time he wants an answer and is focused hard on my eyes as I pull off the helmet and look back at him. "Um, you mean, uh, before the turn back there?"

"License and proof of insurance, please. Move over here away from the road." I hand over the documents and then continue unwrapping myself from my riding gear. I have the sinking feeling we are going to be here for a while. "In fact, why don't you come with me? Get in the car!" He doesn't say it like he is really asking me if I want to or not. I comply reluctantly, realizing that I am getting later by the second.

As we sit in the car together, he studies my papers. I look up at the dash to see a small red digital indicator flashing 78. He must have gotten me before the turn when I was still off the throttle, setting up for a fast exit. I am almost relieved. He is workmanlike as he begins entering my personal data into his onboard car computer. I am further relieved as I realize that my driving record, up till right now, has been clean and that I haven't had any traffic violations in years. It is uncomfortably quiet in the car as all this is going on. I look over my left shoulder and behind the young trooper's head at the other cars that are now driving slowly by us on the highway apron. The patrol car's roof lights are ablaze, and the nosy passersby are twisting their necks inhumanly and squinting hard to get a look at the action. It would have been funny watching these nutballs contort themselves if it weren't for the sudden jolt of the gravity of the situation as the officer asked another question. "Have you ever been arrested, Mr. Douglas?" Could he actually have found that time in high school when I had the beer in my car on his onboard computer that quickly? "Well, when I was in high school."

"Any other time besides that?" he abruptly interrupts. Apparently he is looking at that offense from my long-ago past. "No, sir," is all I say, wondering what time it is.

"Do you know what the speed limit is through here, Mr. Douglas?"

"Sixty."

"That's right. Where were you going that you had to get to in such a hurry?"

"I'm on my way to work and I'm really running late."

"You are?" he replies, still looking down at his monitor, almost as if to indicate that we might be going elsewhere instead. I wondered, *Could I actually be getting locked up for speeding?* I exercised my right and remained silent.

"You have a very good driving record, Mr. Douglas. It is hard for me to believe that you are so late to cause you to be riding that fast this morning." For the first time since our encounter began, the officer looks up at me with an almost sympathetic expression. "Can you explain that to me?"

Knowing that no explanation is going to be good enough, and again feeling that I am about to be trapped by my own words, I say, "Sir, I do not really have a good explanation for you. I was just enjoying the ride."

"A little too much, don't you think?" He finally cracks a little chuckle. I feel a sudden relief from the pressure he is obviously keeping me under while he evaluates me. "Perhaps," is all I can think of to say.

"Well, I've got to give you a ticket."

Got to? Look, it would be all right with me if you just give me a stern tongue lashing and let me get going. For some reason, however, I don't think it's going to be that way.

Interstate Motorcycles

"I am going to give you a break though, just because you really do have a good driving record. I'm only going to write you for seventy miles per hour in a sixty zone. It isn't any cheaper, but it doesn't reflect as poorly on your driving record. Do you understand?"

What do I look like to you, young man, a complete idiot? Of course I understand. I understand it's going to cost me about two hundred bucks! I understand perfectly. "Thank you, sir, I appreciate that," is all I let actually escape my tightened lips.

After getting the paperwork, some more lecturing, and the proverbial "Have a nice day," I am on my way again. I only thought I was running late before; it is eight thirty. Now I am only going to be able to go straight to work and get bikes and products moved into open-for-business position. I usually get to the store between eight and eight thirty and well ahead of service manager Adam Bower, who usually rolls in right on time at about nine. As I pull onto the rear parking lot, I see Adam is already there and moving things around to open the store. Seeing me, he gives me a concerned, long look. It's very unusual for him to get there ahead of me unless I've told him in advance that I will be late.

"Everything all right?" he asks me as I enter the rear service department door. "Yeah, everything is okay. I'll tell you all about it later." The service area is neat, clean, and well ordered, which is how both Adam and I insist that it be kept. The floor is swept corner to corner and mopped cleaner than many highway diners. Bikes being worked on are on lifts, raised to eye level in predesignated stalls. Customers' bikes are parked in neat rows on the back side of the service department, safely stored until we can perform whatever work they await. The ceiling fluorescent lighting is overdone, making the entire work area as bright as an operating room.

I cut through the parts department on my way to my desk, where cardboard and plastic bins sit on rows of shelves, each bin containing parts as large as tires, gas tanks, and even full chassis, down to tiny special screws, washers, and other fasteners. The department is swept and dusted regularly by Lori, who insists on keeping the area neat. Once out to the showroom where my desk is located, I stop momentarily to survey the room. We try to keep it as though it were our very own home, awaiting company to come for a visit. The shelves are neatly arranged and constantly adjusted so that even if a helmet has been tried on by a dozen different heads, it looks like it just came out of the box a few minutes earlier. Apparel is displayed in rows on either floor racks or on the bright slat-board walls around the shop on bright chrome cascades. The two are checked and rearranged daily so that every zipper is up to the collar and every snap is fastened. Oils and cleaners are located separately and near the parts/service counter, where customers can look through and select just the right products for the two-wheeled magic carpet that belongs to them as we write up their repair orders. In a separate corner, neatly mingled in with the new motorcycles parked in tight rows around the floor, is a customer waiting area where there is a wall-mounted flat-screen television showing recorded motorcycle racing all year round. Lighting throughout the showroom is done with lots of large windows and cool white fluorescent fixtures, giving the entire place a warm but spacious look that makes it easy to want to hang around in. And the entire showroom floor is a highly polished, slick, finished concrete that is swept with a wide dust mop several times a day, mopped at least weekly, and commercially waxed several times a year. The phone starts ringing immediately. It is my insurance agent's office calling to remind me that I had made arrangements to drop off a check first thing this morning. *Are they kidding me?* "I'm just running a little behind this morning, Martha. I have the check right here in my hand and will get over to you as soon as possible."

Interstate Motorcycles

"Well, Ray is going to be right over by you in a few minutes." Ray is my insurance broker. "Would you like for me to call and have him stop by to pick it up?"

"That will be fine. Just let him know that I haven't been by the bank yet today either, and I have to make yesterday's cash sales deposit to cover the full amount."

"I'll tell him."

It couldn't have been more than three minutes before Ray was there. Adam and I were still getting the store open, and of course, Lori wasn't there yet because I had diverted her. So we were just a little frazzled. "Hi, Mike," Ray says from the front door as he comes toward me. "I was just coming passed here when Martha called me from the office."

"Here you go, Ray," I say, handing him both the check and the payment due notice.

"Thanks, Mike. You guys are great customers, and we really appreciate your business."

You could appreciate us a little more if you would give just a little latitude on the due date. "No problem, Ray. Sorry it's right on the deadline."

"That's all right. You have never been late. Listen, you look busy, I'll get out of your way."

I know business is tight for him too. He probably needs his cut of that premium as bad as I need to get some of these service bikes picked up and paid for. "Thanks for swinging by, Ray. See you later."

We just finished putting bikes out front when the phone goes again. "Where's Lori?" Adam asks with a slightly confused look. She usually does all of the phone answering. "Uh, I'll tell you all about that later too."

Adam nods knowingly and heads to the service department. He has been with us now for about four years and has made himself an important part of the activity around here. He's one of the few guys I've ever had in the shop that I totally trust. I admire him too. It's not that he's twenty-five and in his prime, either, though his stocky build and full beard make him look older. It's that he's a natural with the bikes. I always wanted his sort of talent. What's taken me a lifetime of hard work and experience to learn just comes easy to him.

"Interstate Motorcycles," I answer, grabbing at the phone off the sales desk. "Mike? Is this Mike?" an all too familiar voice asks.

"Yeah, it's me." This is one of those moments when I am really sorry that Lori is not here. Had she been here, she would have answered this call and screened this guy out.

"This is Bob Culp. How you doing?"

"I'm doing all right. What's up?" I was short with him, hoping to get to the point quickly so I could say no and get back to work. I've known him for a long time and usually a call like this means he needs some kind of a favor.

"I know you're probably busy. I was just wondering if you were going to be there and if I could drop by to talk to you about something. I've got a business proposition for you."

"A business proposition, what kind of proposition?"

Interstate Motorcycles

"Well, I'd really rather talk to you there, if that would be okay, but what I have will make you some money, if you're interested."

Culp has been a dopehead and a drunk and has been in and out of county jail all of his adult life. He has managed to lose every good opportunity he has ever had, including working for me in the service department on several different occasions, and he's ended up stealing and scamming people to generate some revenue for himself. "Listen, I am not interested in some kind of bull."

"This isn't some kind of bull," he interrupts. "I'm just talking about renting some space from you, to do some repair work of my own. I will pay up front in cash."

Cash up front got my interest. "I don't know, Bob. It sounds wacky to me."

"I could be there in about an hour, and I will explain the whole deal in just a few minutes. If you don't like it, I'll be out of there and that will be the end of it, if that's okay with you."

"All right, I'll see you then. I've got to get busy." "See you then," he says as he hangs up the phone.

I have known Bob for a long time. As a practical matter, he has very few redeeming qualities. He is about six foot, two inches tall with a pale complexion and an unhealthy-looking thin build. The physique is probably more the result of bad lifestyle choices rather than genetics. His long and prematurely gray hair and complete mess of a bearded, semi-toothless, and partially tattooed face all combine to give this guy the two-strike looks of a natural-born loser. The only thing keeping him in the batter's box of life, and the endearing quality that causes me to retain an irrational soft spot in my heart for him, is his

15

gentle voice and truly charming personality. But those are the same strengths that make him a talented conman too. Bob's one, true lifelong goal for himself would be full, patch-wearing membership in an established outlaw motorcycle gang. Unfortunately, he hasn't even been able to achieve that.

With the shop opened, I make my way to my desk in the showroom to check my payables-due file. It is stuffed with unpaid invoices. This whole year, I have been forced to apply a kind of triage approach to our payables. Pull out the bills that are bleeding the most and commit whatever cash I can from sales or from available credit lines to get them paid. Today's biggest problem is the shop's insurance premium of eleven hundred dollars, which, if it were one day late, would result in an automatic policy cancellation. We could reinstate the policy, of course, but that would require an immediate first, last, and current month's premium totaling thirty-three hundred dollars. Operating a motor dealership in Missouri without insurance even for one day is illegal. So the state would have been electronically notified of the cancellation, resulting in an automatic revocation of our dealer's license, effectively putting us out of business. Of course we could reapply for our dealer's license as well, but that would require a new cash surety bond of five hundred dollars plus all associated license fees, plus prior license cancellation penalties. Obviously the insurance premium is today's heavy bleeder, but putting everything I had into the payment means I am going to have about a half a dozen other bills past due. I pull out the latest ones and begin calling the companies to explain my dilemma and make arrangements to do whatever we can to stay in their good graces. If we can get our completed service jobs picked up and paid for today, it would certainly relieve some pressure. But it is December and cold in the Midwest, and most motorcyclists are parking their bikes for the year anyway. People think that since they're not going to ride their bike till spring, there's no harm in leaving it at someone's repair shop. Every year, as winter sets in, it is the

Interstate Motorcycles

same. Lori makes a point of reviewing the completed file every week and calling the owners to remind them their bikes are ready, and they owe us money, but the cold weather effectively removes much of the customers' motivation to get here and settle up. "Hey, Mike," Adam calls from the back door of the showroom. "Do you know your Breva has a flat tire?"

"Hold on for a moment," I implore of the kind young lady in the accounts payable department of our largest parts and accessories supplier. "Yeah, I know," I answer Adam, covering the phone with my palm. "Do you have time to look at it for me?" He nods and exits as line two begins to ring. It is still another vendor who is calling about our due account. While I'm phone-juggling vendors, begging for breathing room, Gene Stanford walks through the front door and boldly strides toward the counter to check out. His jaw is set firm, and his eyes are locked forward. My desk is located on the shop's open showroom floor off to one side and intermingled among three short rows of motorcycles and two long shelving units filled with parts and accessories, all of which we have for sale. I would have risen to intercept him except for the phone on my ear. Gene is so determined to get to the counter and begin complaining that he doesn't even notice me. For us to learn exactly what has failed in his old bike's engine, we will have to remove and dismantle it. When we made this discovery, we contacted Gene to bring him up to speed, but he wouldn't hear it. As it turns out, he just got the motorcycle from an old friend who gave it to him for free, not running, and told him that the engine was fine, that it would only need a good tune-up. Now he is certain we are trying to take advantage of him.

Seeing that I am stuck on the phone, Adam steps up to the counter to ring Stanford out. The counter is located on the opposite corner of the rectangular showroom from my desk, making it impossible for me to hear the conversation between Adam and Gene. From my angle, Gene's back is to me and

17

Bill Dunkus

I can see Adam's face, his eyes shifting back and forth from Stanford's to mine. "Can I get back with you this afternoon?" I ask the accounts receivable clerk on the other side of the phone. "I have a bit of a problem I'm going to have to handle." "That will be fine, Mr. Douglas. My extension is 269."

I take a long, deep breath as I hang up the phone. I really want to compose myself before I bail Adam out, but I am not about to let this guy grind on him for another second. "How are you, Gene?" I say with a firm tone as I approach the counter.

"Well, I'm not worth a darn right now," he snaps back at me. "There wasn't a thing wrong with that engine when I brought it here. Now you're telling me it needs a complete overhaul. What kind of outfit you running here, Douglas?"

It appears that Gene is going to double-down on us. Not only does he not want to pay for the partial service and diagnostic that we have already completed, but now he is laying the blame on us for the engine that clearly has significant internal damage. I shift my eyes back to Adam, who slightly rolls his eyes and shrugs his shoulders as if to say, *I don't know what to tell him.* "Adam, go ahead to the back and get Mr. Stanford's motorcycle out for him." I want my technician off the hook right now. "Gene, how long have you had that Honda?"

"Well, I just got it."

"Have you ever rode it?"

"I rode it here for you to tune up. It was running lousy. That's why I brought it here."

"Has it ever run right since you got it?"

"No!"

Interstate Motorcycles

"Well, that's because you have a dead cylinder."

"Well, what would have caused that?"

"I don't know. Like I told you on the phone yesterday, we will have to dismantle the engine to determine what is causing the compression loss."

"Well, how do I know that you or that boy back there didn't tear up that engine running it around here?"

"Because neither of us have ridden the motorcycle. We simply began the tune-up, as you asked us, and learned while we were on it that it has a bad engine."

"So you say, anyway. I'll tell you right now I don't think I should be paying you for working on the thing when you are giving it back to me just as fouled up as it was."

"Sir," I say drawing in another deep, relaxing breath to keep myself from boiling over, "as I explained to you on the phone, we worked on the motorcycle for about an hour before we realized that we had more to deal with than the simple tune-up that you asked us to perform. We didn't know, nor could we have possibly known when you brought it in, that it needed the extensive work that we know now that it needs. The balance due on you work order is seventy-five dollars, which is significantly less than the job you asked us to do would have cost, had we been able to complete it. However, that cost does represent the time we spent on it for you. Look, at least now you know what you are dealing with and if you think we are trying to pull something over on you, take it to another shop and have them verify it."

"So you are going to charge me the seventy-five dollars?"

He lets the question lay out there like a slow-breaking curveball. He is, at the very least, looking for me to cut the amount to make him happy. I look down at the completed work order in my hand. I know from experience with guys like Gene that he is making me a lose-lose offer. If I charge him the full amount, he won't be happy and he will leave in a huff, probably never do business with us again, and tell all of his motorcycling friends what a lousy shop we are. If I cut the amount to make him happy, he still won't be happy because the motorcycle still needs an overhaul to run properly and he will always associate that with us. We will still probably never get his business back, and he will still tell all of his friends what a lousy shop we are. Plus I will be out the money for our work, which right now I need every penny of. Looking back up and locking eyes with him, I say, "Yes, the bill is seventy-five dollars." "Well, there it is," he fires back as he tosses three twenties, a ten, and a five-dollar bill on the floor. "Where is my bike?"

I mark the work order *paid in full–cash,* tear off the customer copy, and hand it to Mr. Stanford. "Thank you, sir. Your motorcycle is alongside the shop at the service department entry." He's just blowing off some steam, venting at us because his bike's in sorry shape, but knowing that doesn't help ease the sting of the tongue lashing. As he storms out of the building, I bend down and pick up our meager earnings.

As Stanford exits the building, Lori is coming in. She sees Gene outside as she is getting out of her car. "How did that go?" she asks.

"Not too good, but he did pay for the service."

"Well, that's good. You know, if he takes the bike anywhere else, they are going to tell him the same thing."

"I know."

Interstate Motorcycles

"Hey, Mike," Adam says as he comes in again from the service department, "I found this in your tire." He holds up a short, thick roofing nail.

"Great," I answer, taking the offender from him and looking at it with distain. The tire that this little piece of metal has just ruined is an expensive Dunlop Qualifier with only about fifteen hundred miles on it. The factory-recommended repair procedure in a case like this is to replace the tire with a new one, but that was going to cost me a couple of hundred bucks so I ask Adam to pull the tire and patch it. He throws me a salute and heads back to his domain once more.

"What do you suppose he wants?" Lori snaps at me while storming out from the parts counter and burrowing her angry eyes into Bob Culp as he parks his car in front of the store.

"Oh, he called a little while ago. He says he has a business proposal to run by me."

"Oh, brother! That cannot mean anything good, Mike. Be careful around him."

Bob was driving the old Chevy Impala, his only alternative transportation to his mostly broken down Harley-Davidson XL1200. There are three other bodies moving around inside Bob's old gray car, none of whom look familiar to me. Bob exits the driver's door and one of the other three guys gets out from the passenger-side front seat. I watch them approach from alongside a rack of tires in the showroom near a side window where they should not be able to see me so I could try to get a read on them. Bob is dressed typical for Bob, in clothes that look like they should be in the laundry. Something new and highly noticeable for him however is the black denim jacket which has had the sleeves removed. There are no patches or pins on the front of the makeshift vest, and on the back is sewn only the bottom, rocker patch section of what looks to be motorcycle club insignia. It is a white patch with black border and the word "Midwest" embroidered in red letters. This uniform clearly identifies Bob as a prospect, or prospective member, of a motorcycle club. A prospect is only able to wear the lowest section of the club's full insignia, or colors as the full patch is called. The bottom, rocker-shaped patch usually gives the location or chapter of the club that the prospective new member is trying out for full membership in. I am familiar with most of our area's club's colors, but the layout and letter style on Bob's prospect rocker is completely unrecognizable to me.

The guy with him is unfamiliar. He is a large guy, about six foot, six inches tall and weighing a very fit two hundred fifty pounds. He is not shabbily dressed at all in wearing new Levis, well-taken-care-of riding boots and a plain black leather jacket. There are no colors on the back of the jacket and only one small, winged Harley-Davidson patch on the chest. His head is bald and face is shaven except for a thick Fu Manchu mustache and a very small teardrop-shaped tattoo on his left cheek right below the corner of his eye. His large, exposed hands and fingers are completely covered in tattoos and what looks like the top of a slanted swastika is tattooed on the right side of his neck and partially exposed above his jacket's stiff collar. The two of them enter the front door together and then turn and go in separate directions without saying a word. Bob's menacing friend turns toward our display motorcycles as if a potential buyer. Bob's head is on a swivel till he spots me, and then he marches toward me with that little Mona Lisa-looking, disarming smile that always seems to be on his face. "What's up, Boss?" he says, approaching with his hand reaching out for mine. He had tagged me with the nickname *Boss* when he worked here.

"How have you been, Bob?" I answer, shaking his hand.

Interstate Motorcycles

"I've been doing pretty good, I guess, just trying to get by."

"Are you working anywhere?" I pretty well know the answer to the question, but I want to see what he tells me.

"No." At least he answered honestly. "So, what's up?" I am watching his friend out of the corner of my eye and hoping to get this meeting over with quickly.

"This is Chainsaw," Bob says as he points.

With that, the big guy looks up at me expressionless and heads in my direction as if with a purpose. "Good to meet you," Chainsaw says. "Bob tells me you are good people."

"Good to meet you too. So what's this whole business proposal about?"

"Right to the point," Chainsaw replies, still not changing expressions. "I like that." "Can we go to the back?" Bob asks, looking around the showroom as if to say this is a little too public for our discussion.

"Yeah." I lead the two toward our service department. Once there, Bob lays out the plan. "Here's the deal. Chainsaw and I have the hookup to start buying wrecked motorcycles—cheap. We are going to strip them and sell them for parts online. We are hoping to make some serious money doing it, but at this point we don't have the commercial address, sales tax number, or merchants permit needed to process credit card purchases over the Internet. We also ain't got a suitable place or the equipment we might need to do the work. What we want to do is rent the shop space and equipment that you already have and funnel all of our sales through here. We will pay you in advance by the month for the rental, and only work here at night when you are closed. You can be making money while you sleep. Plus we will handle all of the sales ourselves and cut you in for twenty percent of everything we make right off the top."

"You are going to buy wrecked motorcycles, cheap?" I skeptically reply. "Buy them where?" It is just a little offensive that Bob would think I am not aware that what he and his new buddies have in mind is running a chop shop on stolen motorcycles in my house. Bob's eyes dart around, indicating that he is taken back by the immediate bluntness of the question and not really prepared with an answer. "Are you kidding me?" I add incredulously. "Bob," Chainsaw interrupts, "Go out to the car and get my smokes." One of the many initiation rituals for a motorcycle club prospect is that any time a full member gives you an errand to run, you do it without question. Bob turns and heads to his car to get Chainsaw's cigarettes without uttering another word. Chainsaw, seeing that I had correctly diagnosed the deal, is taking over the negotiation. "Look here, Mike, you and I both know Bob is not the smartest cookie in the box, but he thinks a lot of you. He says you've taken care of him when he needed help in the past. I'm the vice president of the Midwest chapter of a club called El Elegido. We are about five hundred members strong with chapters on both the east and west coasts. I moved here from southern Cal about a year ago with a couple of the brothers and we are forming the Midwest chapter now. Bob is one of our prospects. "We are setting up business, with or without you, and you don't need to know where we are buying motorcycles cheap. That's our business. All you have to be is the landlord. We will pay you two thousand a month in cash for use of the facility plus twenty percent of gross sales which you will be able to track easy enough because all of the sales will be through Interstate Motorcycles. You just deposit the cash we give you and process the credit cards, keep your cut, and send our eighty percent on your company check to where we tell you, when we tell you. It's as easy as that. The club has setups like this with retail shops on

Interstate Motorcycles

both coasts and once we get the deal up and running, it's a cash machine—seamless and simple.

"Like I said, Bob thinks pretty highly of you and recommended we run this by you first. We figured since someone around here was going to make some extra cash, it might as well be someone who has looked after one of our guys in the past. You have taken care of Bob, now it's your turn, if you want it."

"What kind of bikes are you, um, buying?"

"Harleys," he says matter-of-factly. "Just Harley-Davidsons, and we ship parts worldwide. We make a lot of money doing this. You might as well get in on it."

"I would like to talk to these other shops you have this arrangement with to see how it goes."

"Negative on that. We go to great lengths to protect the identity of our partner shops, just like we will with you. No one ever knows officially that we are affiliated in any way."

Bob comes and hands Chainsaw his smokes. He can see that I am up to speed on the deal. "This could be a real moneymaker for you and Lori, Boss. You ought to get in on it."

"Think it over, Mike," Chainsaw concludes, handing me a wad of cash. "Here is the first month's rent, just so you know we aren't kidding. If you decide you are not interested then just hand it back to me the next time we see each other. No harm, no foul, and we all part friends. We will be in touch. Let's go, Bob." As they leave, Lori is coming in. "More good news," she says in that tone that let me know this is not going to be good.

"What is it now?"

"The bank called. Ray took the insurance premium check there and asked for cash. They went ahead and covered the full amount although we didn't have it in the account yet. They just wanted to let us know that there was a fifty-dollar service charge for the overdraft. I thought you were going to the bank first thing?"

Looking down, I remain silent for a moment, having one of those almost out-of-body experiences where you wish you were somewhere else, anywhere else. Then I reach into my wallet pocket and remove the small bundle of bills from yesterday's sales rubber banded to the completed deposit slip. I hand it to her and screw on as pleasant of a smile as I can summon. "I didn't make it there. Would you mind taking this to the bank? I can't leave right now. I've got to stay here."

Looking right through me, she sees that I am in distress. "Are you all right?"

"Yeah, I'll be fine."

"What did those two say that has upset you so much?"

"It's not them. The whole day is off to kind of a rough start. I'll tell you about it when you get back."

"Are you sure you are going to be okay?"

"Yeah, really, everything is going to be fine." After she turns and walks away, I thumb through the cash Chainsaw left with me. There are two thousand dollars even, in fifty—and twenty-dollar bills. Clean, tempting, and untraceable. It is enough money to square my past-due bills from last month and get me back on the tracks for this month in time to close out the year without having to beg the bank for additional credit. Could this new income be the answer to my prayers? As

Interstate Motorcycles

unlikely as it seems, it dropped right in my lap at just the right time. But is it legal? At this point, I can't afford to care.

I put the cash in an envelope and place it in the top drawer of my desk and try to get back to work. As tempting as it is, I know that as soon as I use that cash, for better or worse, the deal is made and I will have to live with this new venture. A venture I'm not sure is legal and I'm not sure I want to be in, alongside guys who I don't know but already don't like and certainly don't trust. All of these negatives and my better judgment serve to drown out any thought that the Almighty is somehow providing this easy cash flow as an answer to prayer. By day's end, I decide to leave that cash right where it is in the desk drawer until El Elegido shows back up, at which time I shall hand it back to Chainsaw without further discussion. As he said, no harm, no foul, and we will all part friends and that will be the end of it.

The afternoon seems long though. Time drags when you are not busy. Because of the lack of activity, around 4:30 p.m. I turn Adam lose for the day. He rode his motorcycle into work this morning as I did, taking advantage of the unseasonably warm day. But now the temperature is dropping fast. It will be dark before he gets home and will probably be an uncomfortable ride. I offer him the service truck to drive but he turns it down. He has good all-weather riding gear and enjoys riding as much as I do, and he wants to ride as much as possible before it turns too cold. Since he is leaving early and we aren't busy in the showroom, Lori leaves about the same time so she can run by the grocery store. I man the shop solo for the last couple of hours of the day. I wipe the dust off helmets on the shelves, polish bikes on the floor, and sweep up the bathroom to keep myself occupied till closing time. While I wait, I can't help but open the desk drawer and look at the envelope full of small denominations, but I don't pick it up. Somehow not touching it makes it easier not to want to keep, but I look at that envelope a dozen times.

Biding her time till evening at supper, Lori opens the subject we have busily avoided all day asking. "What did Culp want this morning?" Her tone made no attempt at disguising her distrust.

I draw a long deep breath to focus my thoughts on the day's trials and tribulations so I can talk to her about it. "He has a business proposal for us."

"Business? What kind of business proposal could that hustler have in mind?"

"He is hooked up with a new club in the area. Culp and the club want to rent space in the service area at night."

"While we are closed?"

"That's right. They claim to be buying wrecked motorcycles to strip for parts. Then they sell the parts online. They are looking for an established dealership to funnel the sales through for a percentage of the gross."

"Sounds like they are looking for cover to run stolen motorcycle parts through," she says, taking a sip of the red table wine we're sharing. "How much money are they trying to tell you is in it for us?"

"Two thousand a month upfront plus twenty percent of the sale price on all of the parts. The sales will come through us, utilizing our credit card processing and bank account, so we will actually handle all of the money. Then we will pay them out their eighty percent and charge it off as costs of goods sold." She flashes me one of those looks that don't need any words,

Interstate Motorcycles

immediately recognizing the deal for what it is: a gangster outfit stealing motorcycles and selling them off as parts and are shopping for a legitimate dealer to flush the cash through. The only thing she says, however is, "They probably don't even have two thousand bucks."

"Funny you should say that. They left me with two thousand in cash today as earnest money."

"You didn't tell them you would do it, did you?"

"No. They left the money to show they weren't kidding and said if we want to proceed it would serve as their first month's rent, in advance."

Before either of us can say anything else, my cell rings. Checking the caller ID intending not to answer it, I see Adam's number. "I wonder what he wants." Adam's wife Teri is on the line. "What's up?" I ask her.

"Mike," she starts out with hesitation, "I wanted to call you to let you know that I don't think Adam will be able to make it to work tomorrow."

What she is saying to me seems odd for several reasons. First, Adam rarely misses work. Second, when he does have to be off, he tells me well in advance and Teri never calls on his behalf. Lastly, neither one of them typically calls me at home for any reason. Hearing Adam in the background complaining in slurred, hardly understandable speech really triggers my confusion. "What's going on, Teri? What happened?"

"I think he wrecked his motorcycle on the way home."

"Where's the bike?"

"It's here. Somehow he managed to ride it here. His helmet is all scratched up and I think he has a broken arm. It's swollen really bad and he can't move it."

"When did it happen?" I say jumping up from the table and startling Lori.

"He got here about an hour ago. He is like in a daze or something. He's not making any sense and when I tell him we need to go to the hospital he just starts cussing and says he isn't going."

"He just got home an hour ago? He left the shop a couple of hours ago. The crash must have knocked him out."

"I don't know," she says, unable to hold back the tears any longer. "He keeps talking about a deer or something. He is not making any sense."

"I'm on my way. Try to keep him still." I'm no physician, but it sounds like he must have taken a severe blow to the head and is now in shock. "His dad is on his way over already."

"Good. I'm coming over too."

"What happened?" Lori asks as soon as I hang up.

"Adam hit a deer." Deer strikes are common this time of year around here. They are almost always fatal for the deer, but when they involve a motorcyclist they can often be fatal for the rider as well.

"Is he all right?"

"Doesn't sound like it. I think he must be in shock or something. I've got to get over there and see if I can help out."

"I'm coming with you."

"Okay, but hurry."

I filled Lori in on what Teri had managed to tell me by phone as we make the twenty-minute trip to Adam and Teri's house. When we arrive, there are already a couple of cars in the driveway and I can see Adam's mangled Moto Guzzi parked near his back door. As we pull into the driveway, Adam's mom comes out the back door. I don't know her very well but we have met a few times. All I know about her for certain is that she doesn't like motorcycles very much. "How is he doing?" I ask.

"The ambulance Teri called got here about the same time we did. He passed out and started having a seizure as the paramedics were trying to convince him to go to the hospital."

"Seizure?"

"They put him on a breathing apparatus and are transporting him to the county medical center. A helicopter is waiting there to life-flight him to St. Louis to a neurological trauma center. His dad and Teri are already on their way to St. Louis to meet him there. I stayed to watch the baby." She began to sob.

Lori and I both put our arms around her, and then I turn to survey the bent-up bike while Lori continues to stroke her and tell her it will be okay. The 850 Moto Guzzi T3 headlight is crushed and the instrument cluster is gone. The slightly twisted front forks and bent fender still bear the short brown, bloody hair that confirms my conclusion of the crash. It was a deer strike and now the full misery I've experienced today has spilled over onto Adam and his young wife as well. I hope he really is going to be okay.

December 2, 2009

It is a cold start to the day as I unlock the front door and change the sign to open. The temperature, which just yesterday had been warm enough to ride in, won't get above the midtwenties. The gusting northerly winds are making it even worse. The whole day is gray, which is pretty much how I feel too. The last update I have on Adam was late last night from the hospital where his dad called me to let me know he was semi-conscious and in intensive care. He asked me to pray for him, which I tried to do through the sleepless night. Although I really just want to sit behind my desk and sulk, I shift myself into autopilot and start going through the motions to get the shop open for business, moving motorcycles out front and arranging the showroom floor for customers I hope will soon be pouring in. Lori arrives about that time, which is earlier than she usually gets in, but without Adam to help get things going she came to fill in the gap. I can always count on Lori. The phone starts ringing immediately, as if callers somehow know she has just arrived. She flashes me a smile and takes a seat behind the sales desk telephone.

Interstate Motorcycles

Almost right on her heels, Culp and his buddy Chainsaw pull onto the parking lot. Both Lori and I had forgotten completely about these guys and their proposition since Adam's accident. They were quickly out of the car and heading inside out of the cold, whipping wind. "Morning fellas," I greet them as they come in. "Cold enough for you today?" Neither of them seems to be in the mood for joking or small talk.

"Morning, Boss," Bob answers.

"Well," Chainsaw chimes in with a long pause, shrugging his broad shoulders.

"Well?" I reply with a disbelieving tone. "Well, what?"

"Are you in or out," Chainsaw snaps back. "You know what I'm talking about. We have got to get things moving and the question you've got to answer is not all that difficult. So, are you in or are you out?"

"Hey, look man, I haven't been able to focus on the deal. My man Adam clipped a deer with his bike last night on his way home. He's in intensive care fighting his way out of a coma."

"You're kidding me?" Bob asks with his eyes bulging. He and Adam had become friends when they worked here together. "Is he going to be all right?"

"We don't really know anything else yet. The last update I got was from his dad last night. He asked us to be praying for him. It doesn't really sound too good."

"Sorry to hear about your man," Chainsaw says. "That doesn't change anything between us though. I've got to get to a club meeting in Los Angeles today. The southern Cal brothers called in the meeting to hear about our progress out here, and I

33

need to tell them if we have a dealer ready to do business with. So . . ." He pauses again with shrugged shoulders and an angry scowl, staring a hole through me.

"Mike." A soft voice interrupts the tension from behind. "You are going to want to take this call," Lori says, her eyes filled with a blend of fright and disbelief.

"Is it about Adam?"

"No, it's the bank. You'd better take it."

"Let me grab this real quick," I tell the two as I point toward the coffee. "Get some coffee on me and we'll get lined out when I'm finished. It will only take a minute." I could tell by Lori's behavior that the call was serious. I quickly get on the phone with my long-time banker Blaine Perry. Blaine is the vice president of commercial banking for the US Bancorp branch that we have all of our business accounts with. The many years we have done business together have fostered a real friendship as well. "How are you, Blaine? What's up?"

"Mike, I've got some bad news for you. I wanted to come out to see you face to face but I am locked up with meetings here at the bank all day today and tomorrow and I wanted to let you know as soon as possible. As you know, your loan on the business property there and your business line of credit are both going to mature at the end of the year. We have been working on renewing those accounts for you here on our end for the upcoming new year. The bank, however, has decided not to renew. It's a corporate move and it's outside of my control. I'm really sorry, Mike. I've done all I could."

My brain seems to lock up. I was going to call Blaine later today and ask him to increase our credit line because I need additional working capital to pay this month and next months

Interstate Motorcycles

bills while cash flow is slow for the winter. "What did you say?"

Blaine clears his throat. I can tell he is having as much difficulty giving me this news as I am having receiving it. "I've got bad news for you. I wanted to come out to see you face to face."

"I heard it, Blaine!" I shout into the phone, interrupting him before he could give me the canned speech again. "What I want to know is how this can be? We have done business with you and US Bancorp for sixteen years now and never missed a payment. Never! We have always been stellar business customers for the bank, even through the last couple of years during a killer recession. So, Blaine, what I'm asking you is, *what the hell are you saying to me?"*

"Mike, I know this hits you like a cheap shot in the gut, but it's not about you. The bank's lending philosophy has always been very conservative and is becoming even more so because of the country's current financial condition. The bank is pulling back on small business lending nationwide. You are just getting caught up in that pullback and it is not because of anything you have failed to do. You have always been a valued small business in this bank branch's portfolio, and a good friend, but corporate has made the move away from small business altogether. I'm really sorry. I will fax over the payoff amounts later this morning."

"Just like that, Blaine? The payoffs on the two notes has to be nearly five hundred thousand. Are you telling me that I have a little over three weeks to come up with five hundred thousand dollars?"

"If you can come up with some kind of a plan, I will do everything in my power to help you."

As much as I want to take Blaine's head off right then and there, I know that it genuinely is not his doing. I had been hearing from small business people throughout the area and across the country who received similar financial news throughout this past year, but I didn't expect to get it. Because we have always kept our affairs in order with our bank, I just never considered it an upcoming problem. I inhale deeply and hold the breath, feeling my heartbeat gradually slow down in my chest. "Whew. Well, thanks for letting me know right away," I calmly say. "Let me try to get my thoughts together. I'll call you back later today or tomorrow and we will come up with a plan. Okay?"

"I'm really sorry, Mike."

"I know. I know you are. Just one thing you can do for right now."

"Sure, what's that?"

"Just don't say Merry Christmas when you hang up, okay? It's not looking too merry right now, you know?"

"I'll talk to you later, Mike." The line clicked and went dead.

I set the phone back down in its cradle and look over my shoulder at the two outlaw bikers standing in the center of the showroom, striking an impatient pose and still staring hard at me through the open office door. I turn and walk toward them seemingly in slow motion, almost as if being dragged by some strange, magnetic force. As I prepare to speak, it seems weird, as though I am not even saying the words, but that they are being said for me by an outside authority using my mouth. Maybe it is a third party consisting of conditions and events far larger and more unstoppable than I could ever conceive. A

Interstate Motorcycles

force bearing down on me, requiring me to make decisions that in reality aren't decisions at all, but foregone conclusions that I have to consciously embrace, whether I like them or not. I've always tried to run a straight business, completely above board and in full compliance. As I close in on Culp and Chainsaw, I survey the store I own, the business I have spent a lifetime trying to build into an honest living for Lori and myself. The lights suddenly don't seem as bright as they once were. The chrome on the motorcycles that surround me seems a little dull. The color seems to be running out of the place right before my eyes. I extend both forearms, parallel to the floor with clinched fists and both thumbs pointing upward. "We're in," I tell the two.

"Cool, the cash is yours" Chainsaw says, bumping his fist into mine. "I will get in touch with you as soon as I get back from LA, and we will get started. Let's go, Bob." They both head out the door. As he exits, Culp turns back to make eye contact. "This will work for you, Mike," he says, but his eyes seem to betray him, almost as if he too is surprised that I actually said yes.

Lori looks sadly toward the floor, watching the drama unfold and understanding the circumstances driving my decision. I know it still breaks her heart. "We need the income," I tell her before she says anything.

"Maybe so, but this has *bad deal* written all over it! I can't really believe you are going along with this nonsense. You know these clowns are up to no good and they are dragging us into it."

"I'll handle these guys. I don't want you to worry about it."

"I sure hope you're right. What are we going to do about the bank?"

"We are going to have to find another bank to put our business with."

"Who?" she asks, hoping I would have a good answer.

"I don't know. We are going to have to get on the phone and start setting up some meetings as soon as possible. I don't think there is any way we will be able to get something set up in the few weeks left in this year, but if we can let Blaine know we are making some progress I think he can get us some more time. That's about all we can do."

"I'll get on the phone and see what I can get going," Lori says as she stands up and walks back toward the business office. I grab her by the arm, spin her around, and put my arms around her. She embraces me back and we quietly hold onto each other for a minute. "We will work it out," she whispers to me reassuringly.

"I know," I answer, not really sure I believed it. "We always do."

She gets into her office and starts researching local banks while I sit down in front of the stack of outstanding bills that need to get paid first. Yesterday's meager receipts are just enough to cover what is most overdue today, so I start writing checks. Once all the bills are ready, I bundle our actual income along with el Elegido's cash, add a deposit slip, and head out to the bank and post office, leaving Lori to watch the shop alone. Customer traffic is, for the moment at least, nonexistent, so I know she will be all right till I get back. The snow is just beginning to fall from those heavy gray clouds.

Interstate Motorcycles

We will be able to get through the month with the assistance of the new revenue, and that seems to dial back the pressure a bit. Enough at least that I can actually start to think again and remember some things as I drive. I start recalling the banks that had stopped by to visit our shop in the last few years and let us know they were interested in our business. I had always turned them down, completely confident that we had a lifelong relationship with our bank. While all of my energy is focused like a laser beam on finances, Adam suddenly pops into my head. He is not only a guy who works here with me in our service department, but he is also a friend. I realize that, while being swept up into the bad news of today that had absorbed me. I had not paused to say a little prayer for him. It was obvious that he had taken a severe blow to the head in the wreck and the consequences of his injuries are as of yet uncertain, but it is conceivable that they could be long lasting or even fatal.

All right, God, are you watching this? Can you see what's going on down here or what? Really? We've got Adam in intensive care, his young wife and family crying out to you for a little help. You see Lori and me losing everything we have spent our entire lives trying to build. We have always played it straight, always did it by the book. Hell! We tried to do it by your Book. When I ask you for some guidance, you send me a couple of gangsters with a wad of cash? Really? So that's it? Are you listening? Are you really even there?

The snow that was just beginning as light flurries when I left the shop is now falling heavy, accumulating rapidly and blowing up into high drifts alongside the road in the stiff winter wind. I really had barely noticed how inclement the day was turning and how dark it had gotten while I was out driving because I was deeply engaged in my own thoughts.

Barley noticed, that is, until I make the last turn onto the long straight stretch of road leading me past the truck stop and back to Interstate Motorcycles. The road is now completely covered with snow and packed down hard by the passing of several heavy trucks. I am on it and sliding sideways before I realize the hazard. I manage to counter-steer the sliding truck and get it stopped, pointing sideways toward the guardrail but still safely on the road. As I stop, a snow-covered guy jumps up from the far side of the guard rail out of a deep snow drift right in front of my headlights. I hadn't seen the guy at all while I was sliding. He gathers his bearings and looks back at me.

"Are you all right?" I shout to the startled pedestrian as I leap out of the cab of the truck. "Yeah, I think so," he says softly, brushing the snow off of himself. "I heard you sliding, then looked back to see you coming right at me, so I jumped across the rail. I didn't realize how much snow was over there till I was in it."

Most people would be righteously enraged at nearly being run over by a sliding pickup truck with a distracted driver at the wheel causing them to jump into a four-foot deep, fluffy snow drift, but this guy was smiling. A small kind of man, about five foot, six and what appeared to be a very slender build under the thick, hooded winter suit he was in. As I came to him, he pushed back the hood which was full of snow and now it was on his neck and under his collar. Still his gentle face had a calm, peaceful smile on it against the driving December wind. "Come here," I say helping him brush off and taking him by the elbow while he crawls back across the rail and onto the highway shoulder. "Get in the truck and get warm."

"Well, I think I might take you up on that."

Interstate Motorcycles

We both hop into the truck and I shift it into gear and begin maneuvering myself back into the direction I was originally pointed. "Where were you at? Where were you going?"

"Well, I just got into the truck stop over here a little while ago," he tells me, pointing with his thumb back at the truck plaza we were alongside of. "I saw a little motorcycle shop on the outer road back here as we were getting off the highway. It looks like they might be a Moto Guzzi dealer and I was just going to walk down there and look around."

"It's about a mile. That is where I'm going. You want a lift? So, what do you ride?"

"I've got an older model Harley-Davidson."

"Really, what model?"

"It's a 1976 FLH Police Special."

I managed to get the front wheels of the pickup pointed back down the road the way I wanted to go. "I own the motorcycle shop you seen back there, and we're a Moto Guzzi dealer. You still want to come down for a visit after I nearly ran you down?"

"Of course I still want to come in." Removing his glove, he thrusts his right hand at me and introduces himself with a friendly ear-to-ear smile. "I'm Kat. Kat Stevens."

"Kat Stevens?" I ask with a smirk as I grab and shake his hand. "My name is Mike Douglas."

"Yeah, my real name is Carl, but with a last name like Stevens, you know someone is always going to call you Cat, you know, like the pop/folk singer from the seventies? Except,

I spell it with a K. I guess it's a generational thing, but the name stuck on me."

"I like it. Let's get you to the shop where there is some real heat," I say as I click the truck into gear and begin easing, a bit more carefully this time, toward my shop. "Your rig safe back there on the lot for a little while?"

"Oh, yeah, it's safe. It's not my truck. I hitched a ride with a privateer, husband and wife team that I met in New York where I lost my last driving job. The company I've been with back east for nearly ten years just folded. It was a small outfit and they just could not keep it going in this economy any longer. I found another company to drive for luckily enough, but they are headquartered on the west coast in Portland, Oregon. I have to get out there and pick up my rig to get started. The husband and wife have a load to pick up in Columbia tomorrow that they are hauling to Portland so they let me to tag along."

As we pull into the lot at the shop, I can see Lori through the window in the showroom with a couple of young guys who are looking at sport bikes. "I sure hope those guys are buyers," I think out loud as we park the truck. "Sales kind of slow for you?" Kat responds.

"Slow! More like nonexistent."

"They'll get better."

We enter the shop together and I introduce Kat to my wife. I briefly tell her how we just met, trying to stay out of her way while she is working with the two young guys. "They are just dreaming," she whispers to me. She was right, as always, and a moment later they were headed out the door. "So you practically ran over this guy," she then says with a big smile as she joins Kat and me by the coffee pot. As we chat and sip

Interstate Motorcycles

coffee together to warm up, he does a quick double-take on the perfectly lined-up row of shiny new motorcycles parked in the showroom. "There it is," he says slowly, turning and stepping in the direction of the bikes. "That is the one I was hoping you would have. I've only seen photos of them. I've never actually seen it up close and in person."

I am not surprised by his choice. Being the owner of an older, vintage motorcycle, this thing was literally designed and built with him in mind. It is solid black and chrome, Moto Guzzi California Vintage. The bike is built very reminiscent of the older model Guzzis like the Ambassador and the Eldorado of the early seventies, with hard saddlebags, tombstone-style windshield, large chrome engine guards front and rear, and running boards. Accenting the deep gloss paint are the flashes of chrome from the engine, fenders, and exhaust and tasteful and artfully applied white pinstriping. He circles it like a hawk hunting prey, salivating. "Do you like it?" I ask after allowing him a moment to take it all in.

"Oh, yes. Yes, I do. How does it sound?"

Without saying another word, I key the switch on and lightly thumb the starter button. She springs to life. Kat's eyes are cemented to the bike as the eleven-hundred-cubic-centimeter v-twin engine idles in an even, smooth cadence, emitting a deep, throaty note from the mufflers. I enjoy watching him admire the motorcycle. It brings to mind all of the reasons I love being in this business in the first place. It sure isn't because it is making me rich. A wise old motorcycle dealer told me a long time ago that the best way to make a small fortune in the motorcycle business is to start out with a large one. But for just a moment, I let all of the pressures, trials, and tribulation of trying to stay in business in the current economic climate slide past me. Momentarily forgotten as well is the mountain of debt we were going to have to try to find a new bank to carry.

Forgotten are the gangsters I am entering into a relationship with to try to keep my business afloat. Forgotten is the piling snow and frigid temperatures outside that are further keeping customers and their money away from my store. I just pause and take in this guy and this machine, beginning a relationship the way only a genuine gear-headed enthusiast does when he first encounters the motorcycle of his current lust. It's almost *sweet*. Like watching two teenagers with their hands all over each other, falling in love while they're trying to figure out what falling in love even is.

"You should own this motorcycle, Kat," I say, reaching my hand into the magic and keying off the engine. Kat's body leans slowly, just a few inches back away from the new Guzzi as his eyes break their lock with the thing and roll downward toward the floor, "Yeah. How much?"

"Fifteen thousand."

"Too rich for me," he replies, screwing a little smile back on his face and taking the throttle into his hand. "Maybe someday though, and I promise I will buy it here when the time comes." I know he means for that to make me feel better, but somehow the promise of a sale to an unemployed, itinerant truck driver in the process of relocating to the opposite side of the country doesn't really ease today's financial pressure. "Thanks for letting me see it. I better be getting on my way. The couple I'm riding with thought I was crazy for coming down here in this weather anyway. They'll be thinking I'm frozen out here in the snow somewhere."

"Listen, it's about closing time for us. If you can wait a little, I'll drive you back up there when I leave."

"You don't mind?"

Interstate Motorcycles

"I drive right by there anyway. That is, if you don't mind hanging around here?"

"Mind? Mind hanging around a motorcycle shop? No, I don't mind at all."

"Well, look around and make yourself at home."

"If you got it from here," Lori says as she comes through her office door and joins me in the showroom next to the Cal Vintage, "I'm going to head out. I need to stop by church."

"See you at home."

As Lori leaves, a car pulls onto the darkened, snowy parking lot out front and a short stocky figure emerges and trots in through the weather and into the store. A smallish guy with full beard and long greasy hair, wearing shiny black denim trousers, a thick, black leather motorcycle jacket, and sunglasses even though it is dark outside. We nod to each other as he enters and starts looking around. On the back of the jacket are the full El Elegido colors. It's the first time I've seen the full patch. The top rocker-shaped patch spreads across his shoulders, bearing the club's Spanish name. The bottom rocker simply reads "Midwest," and in the center is what appears to be a severed human head with eyes tightly clinched, mouth agape, and hanging from some sort of a stick by its own hair. What the gruesome image has to do with motorcycling, I cannot figure out. "Can I help you find anything?"

"Just looking. I'm a friend of Chainsaw," he replies in a deep baritone voice with a thick Texas accent. "I just stopped in to check the place out."

"I can't help noticing that Kat's demeanor changed as soon as this guy showed up. He seems to be making a point of steering clear of the guy, all the while keeping an eye on him. The Elegido finishes a slow ramble around the showroom touching helmets, jackets, and handlebars but not picking anything up for close examination. "See you around," he mumbles as he exits back to his car. "Is he a regular?" Kat asks, watching him drive off through the front windows.

"It's a long story. Did you know that guy?"

"No. I just know the type."

I get the place closed up and conclude another long, disappointing day. Total sales in the till around thirty-five dollars for a couple of spark plugs and oil filters Lori sold. I guess it's better than nothing, but not much. Kat and I ease over the snow-covered road back to the truck stop where I picked him up earlier."What do you know about El Elegido," Kat asks.

"Nothing really, they are new in town. One of the guys who used to work in my service department is prospecting for them."

"Tell him to be careful. You be careful around that bunch too. I'll be praying for you guys and I'll be praying that if those guys just drifted into town that they keep right on drifting out of here," Kat tells me in a serious tone.

"Praying? I didn't figure you to be the praying type. Jesus freak, huh?"

"Well, I guess if you've got to be a freak over something, Jesus is about as good as you can get," Kat answers with a slight tone of indignation and looking out the passenger side window of the truck.

Interstate Motorcycles

"Hey, I didn't mean anything by that. I guess I'm kind of a Jesus freak myself, you know?"

"No offense taken," Kat answers with a slight smile. "I don't mind being called a Jesus freak."

"Which rig you sleeping in tonight," I ask him as we slowly drive along the row of tightly packed tractor-trailer rigs.

"I'm sleeping in the truckers lounge inside," Kat says, cocking his thumb back over his shoulder toward the building. "The berth on the rig only sleeps two, and they are husband and wife, you know."

"How are you going to sleep in the lounge?"

"I'm just going to pull two of those chrome and red vinyl chairs together, curl up on one, and put my feet up on the other."

"No, what I mean is how are you going to sleep with drivers coming and going, the televisions blaring, and the video games dinging all night long?"

"You get used to it. I've done it before."

"I'll tell you what. I know a place where you can sleep in a real bed, in a private room where it will be warm, dry, and quiet and you can get a good night's sleep. Best of all, it won't cost you a dime. I've got two extra bedrooms at my place and we will throw in a meal to boot."

"I can't do that."

"Look, I like you and I can't leave you up here curled up on those crazy chairs in that crummy drivers lounge all night trying to stay warm while I've got two warm, dry unused beds at my place. We do it for customers from out of town who end up stuck here unexpectedly all the time. Besides, it would just be good customer relations. You're going to buy something, someday, right?"

"I don't think I should."

"Sure you should."

"What about Lori?"

"What about her? I'm sure she can throw an extra burger on for you."

We get to the house and I settle him into our extra bedroom. Lori wasn't even surprised. She could tell I liked the guy already, and when I told her where he was planning on sleeping, she was even relieved that I didn't leave him there. "I'm sure he won't be any trouble for one night," is all she says.

"I really want to thank you both. I don't know how I can repay you," Kat tells us as we sit down for supper.

"You don't owe us anything," Lori responds.

"Well, I just want you to know I really appreciate it. Your home is beautiful and your hospitality is very unusual these days. Thank you."

"Don't mention it."

"So, where do you guys go to church?" Kat asks.

"What?" I ask. The question seemed a bit random.

Interstate Motorcycles

"Lori said she was going by the church when she left the shop, and you said you were kind of a Jesus freak, so I was just wondering, where do you guys go to church?"

The matter has been just a little contentious in our house these days. Lori is the treasurer at our church and extremely active. I, on the other hand, have become increasingly distant from church, not as if some earth-shattering event has driven me away but more of just slow-growing atrophy. It troubles Lori that I've been fading out lately, but we don't argue over it. She just keeps reminding me that I *used* to be more involved. "We worship at the First Church of God in St. James."

"When you still actually go," Lori answers with a sarcastic smile.

"I go," I say to sidestep the comment. "How about you, Kat, where do you go?"

"Well, it's kind of tough in my line of work. I'm never really sure where I'm going to be on Sunday mornings. I keep an ear to my rig's CB to find out where the mobile trucker's church is going to be. They are a group that operate small trucks which travel around the country to various truck stops and rest areas along the highways, setting up makeshift chapels for services. If I'm anywhere near where I hear they are going to be, I go to church with them. That is about the best I can do. All of the years I've been a believer, I've driven a truck driver. I've never been a part of a regular permanent church family. It must be good to have a regular church home."

"It is," Lori answers for us both. "We should count our blessings," she says, flashing me a warm smile.

"Yes, we should," I answer her with a gentle, affirmative nod. "I have been less than regular at our church home lately,"

I conclude, addressing Kat directly. "Why is that?" he asks with a puzzled look.

It was a good question, but there was not a short answer. When you are in a small business that deals directly with the public such as mine, you unfortunately get a hard look at the darker side of people. It has been demoralizing to me over the years to meet people in my shop who lead off by telling me about their faith upfront and then immediately make every attempt to take advantage of me. Sometimes it is by outright fraud or dishonesty and other times it can only be described as theft. Often they just try to squeeze me out of my products and services and pay little or even nothing for them. One perfect example was the experience I had just the previous day with Gene Stanford, who first asked us to do a minor repair on the motorcycle that needed a major overhaul and then accused us of trying to cheat him when we gave him the bad news about his engine. Reverend Stanford is the senior pastor of a nearby Baptist church, although it would be tough to believe it by his behavior in public. I have a feeling that my store and I will be used in a negative illustration during an upcoming sermon. Or the countless times I have had believers in here tell me specifically, "Yes, I will buy that motorcycle. Get it ready for me. I will be right back with the money." Then we never see them again. Or the guys who are my best friends and brothers in the faith who are always at our shop for a promotional day when I'm giving away prizes, free food, and soda pop and who always know how to find me when they need a financial commitment for some good cause their church is doing but make a point of buying their motorcycle parts and accessories elsewhere if they think they can save a few dollars. Or the guys who stink the place up the most when they bring in motorcycles that they bought elsewhere to begin with, then rack up whopping repair bills at my shop as they turn their bargain-basement bikes into something they can actually ride, then stiff me on the bill. A couple of these jokers actually go to the same church that Lori

Interstate Motorcycles

is so involved in and that I have slipped away from. It is pretty hard for me to have these guys approach me at church on the Lord's day and want to make small talk but never open the subject or make any attempt to pay me the money they owe us. Not a single dime. "I've just been awfully busy," is all I answer.

"You're not slipping away from the faith, are you?" Kat asks bluntly.

"No, it is not like that at all. I am as committed as I have ever been to following Jesus. I am just not too interested in . . ." I pause, searching for just the right words to describe my thoughts. "I'm not very fond of the way I see others behave, sometimes, in the name of Christ."

"People getting under your skin a little, huh?"

"I guess you could say that."

"Well, Mike, I don't know who has stepped on you or what they did, but you have to remember that they are just human beings. Becoming a Christian doesn't make them perfect, just forgiven."

"I know all of that," I answer before Kat can completely finish the sentence. "Trust me, I know all of that. Least perfect of all is me. Ask Lori." I nod toward my wife.

"Well, you may not be perfect," she answers without hesitation, "but you're just right for me." Then she leans from her chair and kisses me sweetly, rising to begin clearing off the table.

Before Kat can say anything else, I add, "Listen, I have been a follower and a believer of Jesus Christ since I was a kid. I have made it a point to be forthright with people and honest and as generous as I could be. I have always believed that if someone truly realizes the enormity and the generosity of the gift that God's salvation represents to all mankind, and really believes in it, then the person who receives that gift should reflect that same generosity in his or her own life to the very best of their individual ability. I am not just talking about chipping in to the collection plate at church either. I believe that how we conduct ourselves in the world, and especially in the marketplace, should reflect an unusual generosity. But what I have found in business is that nine out of ten times if a customer of ours is trying to pick my pockets, he is probably claiming to be Christian, doing it in the name of the Lord."

"Wow," Kat answers after a short pause. "I can see that you have been hurt a lot by a lot of people. I'm sorry to hear it."

"Don't be sorry. It's no big deal. It's just what people do. My beef isn't with God or even with nonbelievers. It's with the people who claim to be godly, churchgoing folk. You know the type who don't smoke, don't consume alcohol, and wouldn't say a cuss word if you squeezed their ear with a pair of pliers. But if they can stiff a waitress out of a tip they are glad to do it. It makes me sick. I can barely stand to see it anymore."

"Could it be that the people that offend you just can't afford to do any better? I mean, I don't have much to give either."

"No, Kat, I'm not referring to guys who are having a tough go of it and just can't do any better. I'm not talking about hard-working guys like you who are just trying to keep body and soul together through the toughest recession of the last half century. I'm talking about people who could do better, and probably should do better, but make it a point to be cheap every chance they get, even if the people that they say they care about get hurt so they can save themselves a pocketful of change."

Interstate Motorcycles

"Maybe they just don't know any better. I'm not trying to defend bad behavior, but maybe they just don't know what they're doing. You know Mike, I don't know about you, but for myself I can tell you that before I became a Christian I was really a bad guy. You wouldn't have invited me into your home if we had met back then. I meet many people who are part of the faith now that have been in the church their whole life. I get the feeling from many of them that they have almost lived a sheltered life. They don't know what really bad behavior looks like. They think that if they just avoid a few accepted Christian notions of behavior, like you said don't drink, smoke, or swear, then they are all right and everything else they do doesn't really matter that much."

"I don't know. I think they know right from wrong."

"Deep down they probably do, but the more someone engages in poor habits, the more acceptable those poor habits have a tendency to become. Listen, I can tell you a person can accept some pretty ugly things about themselves if they engage in it long enough.

"I'm not proud of it," Kat went on, pushing the sleeves of his sweatshirt up, "but I can tell you from my own experience that a person can fall into some pretty lousy lifestyle choices without even realizing it's going on."

Kat's exposed arms revealed more tattoos than skin, starting at his wrists. "I can remember the first motorcycle I ever laid eyes on. I was maybe five or six years old at a little soda shop in Bakersfield, California, where I grew up. There I was, sipping a cherry Coke when three guys pulled in on the most magnificent machines I had ever seen. Two-wheeled magic carpets, loud and flashy, with big guys, probably just teenagers themselves, piloting them. The second my eyes landed on them, I knew I had to have one. I can still feel the tickle on my eardrums from the exhaust note. I can still smell the ninety-weight that was seeping from the transmissions onto the hot exhaust pipes as they sat parked on the gravel while the big guys went inside for a Coke. I stood as close to the bikes as I dared to get and stared in complete reverence. It changed my life forever. I was a biker from then on.

"Motorcycling dominated my every free moment. Every time I heard one passing through the neighborhood, I tried to get a glimpse. Any time I heard the word *motorcycle* my ears perked up. I built plastic models and read books about them to learn everything I could.

"My parents hoped that it was just a phase that I would grow out of. My father hated the things nearly as much as I loved them. He made it crystal clear to me that if one ever came into my possession, I would be disowned by him forever. Even this did not dissuade my passion.

"When I was fifteen, a kid from the neighborhood that I knew who owned a motorcycle told me that I could have his. It was a CL305 Honda. He had just gotten his orders to go to Vietnam and was sure that when he got home from the war he would have enough money to buy a Harley. There was a string attached however. I had to steal the bike from his backyard so he could report it stolen and collect the insurance. I signed up for the operation without hesitation.

"I snuck into the backyard of his parents' home where he lived on the prescribed night, and, just as we had prearranged, the bike was parked on the sidewalk with the key in the ignition, ready to go. The one and only fly in the ointment was that I had never actually ridden a motorcycle before.

"I keyed the thing on, gave it a few good licks on the kick started, and the machine burst to life. All I knew for sure to

Interstate Motorcycles

do was squeeze in the clutch and toe the shifter into first gear, which I did without hesitation. I had to move quickly. I was stealing the thing, you know.

"Well, I released the clutch and *whoosh!* The thing leaped into motion. Then bam, straight through the neighbor's fence! I sideswiped a parked car on the way through and hit the street at full throttle. Wow, what a ride.

"I remember seeing the guy looking out the upstairs window of his parents' two-story home as I zipped away and I don't know if he was laughing or crying while I was tearing up his motorcycle and the surrounding property, pulling off the worst motorcycle heist of all time."But, I was riding, baby! I ran the thing around the neighborhood hoping that some of my friends would see me, but they were all already in bed. The next day was a school day, you know. I worked my way through upshifting the thing and, man, I was really booking. I couldn't have been more thrilled if I had been strapped onto a Titan III rocket and launched at the moon.

"I probably don't have to tell you how this ended, but I crashed the hell out of that little Honda. Hit a tree. Not just any tree, mind you, but the biggest, oldest oak tree in all of Bakersfield, and it did not give an inch. When I regained consciousness, I was already in an ambulance headed to the emergency room with a busted-open head and a severe concussion. The 305 Honda didn't fair much better and was scraped up off the accident scene and transported to the nearest scrap-metal yard. My dad never forgave me.

"I didn't even care. By then I realized that I had always been right about bikes and that they were all I wanted to do from then on. When I got out on my own, I rode any kind of motorcycle I could get my hands on. Anything I could afford. Always hoping to eventually own the bike I thought was the top shelf, number one. Of course it was the big twin Harley-Davidson. When I got into my early twenties, I finally had scraped, saved, and stolen enough to buy a ragged-out, rat-style chopper Harley from an area drug dealer who needed to raise some quick cash for a lawyer to beat a dope-dealing arrest. I had finally made the big time.

"It wasn't long after that that I started hanging at all of the local *biker* bars and making some serious friends in the biker world. Before you know it, I was a prospect for an outlaw club and I thought the world was my oyster."

"It's a great story, but what does it have to do with people who claim Christ while being crooked?" I was curious.

"Well, after getting hooked up with the club, I got into a lifestyle that, although I thought it was what motorcycle guys did, it didn't really have anything to do with motorcycles at all. You know, you can call gangsters anything you want: mafia, Crips, Bloods, Hells Angels, whatever. At the end of the day, they are all just gangsters. Although I started out with the intention of being a serious motorcyclist, I ended up becoming just another gangster, and I didn't even realize that the transition was taking place.

"I think that a lot of these same people who claim Christ as Savior fall into a similar trap. They think that if they show up at church on time every Sunday, don't drink, don't smoke, don't, swear, etc., etc., well, they think that other trash is just all right. They slip out of touch with Christ and end up buying into a load of religiousness. I don't think they even see it.

"Like all of these tattoos, I never wanted a single one of them. I just wanted to ride motorcycles with the group. But I let the peer pressure get to me, and before you know it I was covered in them. And that was just the beginning. It wasn't

Interstate Motorcycles

long and I was doing some really ugly stuff just to stay in good standing with them. I started off with simple little crimes like strong-arm robberies, robbing liquor stores, and stealing cars. Eventually I was cooking meth and participating in contract beatings on clients of bookies, loan sharks, and used car dealers who paid us quite well to extract their satisfaction.

"Those folks that I have met who have had the luxury of being part of the church their whole life probably don't even know the effect they have on a guys like you and me with that crap, guys who are just trying to make a simple living. I think they just gradually slip like I did, but, instead of going from a motorcyclist into a gangster, they morph into a self-serving and self-righteous religious shell. Life and faith becomes all about themselves and less about Jesus. Their focus changes like mine did, maybe like yours has. No offense, but it sounds like you might be a little too hung up on money."

"Hey, look, when you are in business for yourself, you'd better be a little hung up on money. No one is going to take care of my responsibilities for me. It's all on me. So, are you still a member of this club?"

"No, I never really was. I was a prospect for a couple of years but never actually became a full member. If I had, I'm not sure I would have been able to completely separate from them."

"I didn't think you ever could completely separate from outlaw clubs."

"Well, it isn't easy and it always has consequences. I had a wife at the time. I say she was my wife but we weren't legally married. We were married by the club. I don't know exactly what started it, but I had been feeling more and more like the outlaw lifestyle wasn't for me. One morning I woke up at the clubhouse with one more hangover, laying on the floor with one more naked chick that I didn't even know, wondering who my *wife* was passed out with, and I just couldn't do it anymore. I went into the backyard alone, lit a smoke, and started to cry. I felt like I was lost, in a dark place with no way out. I reached out to the only one I thought might really be able to help me. I started praying. I prayed right out loud that Jesus would forgive me. And he did. Something really miraculous happened. I can't explain it any other way. I've never been the same since, and it's not because of some effort I made on my own. Something seemed to drive a change in me from the inside out.

"From that hungover morning on, I've been a believer. There was no doubt I was leaving the lifestyle and I wanted my wife to leave also and ride away with me, but she wouldn't. Maybe she just couldn't. She packed her stuff the next morning and started riding on the back of another guy's bike who was a full member of the club."

"She left you?"

"She just didn't want to leave that whole club scene. The scene was always more important to her than the motorcycling itself. She told me she loved me, but she thought I had gone crazy and that I had become some kind of a Jesus freak."

"Man," I said with heartfelt sincerity, "I am really sorry about calling you that. I didn't mean anything by it."

Laughing, Kat reached out to shake my hand. "I know you didn't, and I hope you won't be offended by the 'hung up on money' comment either."

"No worries, I'm not. So that did it, you were finished with the club scene?"

Interstate Motorcycles

"Well, not quite that easy. Her and her new old man had to let the chapter president, a guy called Spider, know what was going down. He made it official and called for my prospect patch, which I turned in of course, and my bike."

"They kept your motorcycle?"

"Yes, they did. Taking it from me made it official with them. I was through and turning over that old chopper meant I could split without further retribution. I figured it was a good deal at the time. I signed on with a trucking company right after that and have been on the road ever since. I bought the old Police Special that I ride now at an auction on the east coast. It's all original and in really good shape for its age. But, you know those older model Harleys sure need a lot of tender loving care to keep them running right. When I get the chance to ride it, which is limited enough, I just want to light it up and go. I don't want to spend my ride time working on it. Besides that, I think I am due for a brand change anyway.

"I've talked to a lot of motorcycle riders over the years at highway rest areas, restaurants, and truck stops, and Moto Guzzis have always interested me. You just don't see many of them, you know? The one that seriously has my attention now is that new Moto Guzzi, California Vintage."

"It's a beautiful motorcycle. You should own the one on my floor."

"I wish I could. But, well you know, it's a money thing. I need to fork some over to you so I can own it, and I don't have any."

"Yeah, I know how it is. It's always a money thing."

December 3, 2009

Kat and I were out of the house early so I could get him back to the truck stop and together with his ride. We exchange phone numbers, e-mail and mailing addresses, and even part with a little hug around each other's neck. "Be careful out there, man. Hope the new company works out good for you," I tell him.

"I will, Mike. Thanks a lot for everything. I hope business really takes off for you next year."

"Stop in and see us if you ever get in the area, will you?"

"You bet I will."

It is a nice thought, but it is highly unlikely. I glance into the truck's rear-view mirror for one final look at my new friend as he climbs aboard the big Peterbilt, which is fueled, warmed up, and ready to roll.

Interstate Motorcycles

The morning is crisp and cold. Temperatures are still below freezing, but the sky is clear and the sun is shining bright. Lori gets to the shop a couple of hours after I do and the two of us get busy contacting banks to discuss moving our business. The bank we both prefer of all of those on our list is called Community Commercial. It's a small, locally owned community bank with a branch office very near to the shop. They would probably be a better fit for our business than the large nationwide organization we have had our business with all along anyway.

As an added bonus, the commercial vice president, a guy named Dean Macfarland, is an avid motorcyclist himself and a long time customer of ours. He has often reminded me over the years that he would love to have our business. Well, now is his chance. Still, we call most of the other banks in town just to make sure we have all of our bases covered and can cut off our connection to US Bancorp as fast as possible. Before the meeting with Dean, Teri Bower calls the shop with an update on Adam.

"He is doing pretty good—awake and alert—but he is still hurting. The doctors say the seizure was the result of the blow he took to his head when he came off of the bike, and he has a broken right arm that will require surgery. They also said that if he hadn't had a good helmet on, he couldn't have survived it."

"How long will he have to be in the hospital," Lori asks.

"They are going to release him either tomorrow or the next day and schedule the surgery on his arm for a couple of weeks from now when the swelling goes down a little. He wanted me to tell you both he was sorry about not being able to make it to work for a while."

61

"Tell him not to worry about it. It's the slow season anyway. We will work it out. Tell him just to get well, so he can make it back when the season heats up again."

"That is good news," Lori says after we get off with Teri.

"Great news," I answer. "We are due for some."

Lori headed back to her office as the phone started ringing again. I took a seat behind my desk on the sales floor and pulled out the file full of bills for my daily exercise in triage. I take a deep, cleansing breath to gather my thoughts and, as I do, I look from corner to corner in the showroom, surveying the bikes, shelves full of helmets, and racks of riding apparel and gloves and miscellaneous accessories all artfully displayed and awaiting purchase. It is virtually our whole life's work and a source of undeniable pride albeit a micro business. Hardly a speck on the American economy, but it's everything we've got.

"Hugh Petrowski, Entrepreneur." My memory digs up that sign again. "What's an entrepreneur, Dad?" I asked him one Saturday morning as we started our rounds.

"An entrepreneur is a guy who starts a business from nothing, makes it work, and makes a living at it. If he works hard enough and is really lucky, he just might make it big someday."

"Is Mr. Petrowski making it big?"

"Well, he's working on it. He calls his own shots, makes it or breaks it on his own terms and by the work of his hands. I respect a man like Petrowski and I hope someday he does make it big."

Interstate Motorcycles

I always remembered it. My dad was an important man and he respected this guy and this guy was an entrepreneur. I wanted my dad to respect me someday for starting something from nothing and making it work with my own two hands. I wanted it even more after Dad lost his job at the dairy.

Dad was an important man in a business that was no longer viable or profitable. It was the late sixties and early seventies and the country was suffering a bad recession then too. Families on tight budgets were opting not to have their milk delivered to their doors by the reliable old milkmen who had been doing it for decades. People learned they could pick up their milk themselves from any number of retail outlets. It was cheaper and just as fresh. My dad had a little over nineteen years on the job at the dairy when they summarily closed it up one day. With very little warning and no apologies, the gate on the family-owned operation was padlocked and the electricity was shut off and that was that. They never delivered another pint of milk. It never occurred to me that Dad was even capable of crying, but that did it to him. He didn't see me the morning that I watched it happen. He was at the kitchen table in the predawn morning and had the phone pressed to his ear. I was behind him in the dark hallway that led to the back of the house where the bedrooms were. The sound of him on the phone that early in the morning had awakened me and I stealthily eased toward it. I couldn't hear the conversation on the other side, but I knew Dad was talking to someone from the union, trying to hook up a new job somewhere. "What do you mean I'm too old? You know you owe me. I've always looked out for you. I don't want to hear that crap. No! I don't want welfare. I want a job! Food stamps, are you crazy? Look, I don't want to hear anymore of this. No, no more. You guys have got to find me something, and fast! I've got a family here to raise."

He gently placed the handset into the desk phone's cradle when the conversation was over, staring at it as if he were waiting for the phone itself to give some answer that made sense to him. Then he slowly placed his elbows on that table and his face into his large, thick-fingered hands and he began to sob. I didn't really understand it at the time, but something had been taken from him, something he cherished and that in large part made him what he was. Maybe it was his pride or self-respect. I don't know, but I felt like it had been taken from me too, maybe because there was nothing I could do to help him. Silently, with tears dripping off my face, I slipped back down the dark hallway to my room and as quietly as possible crawled back into my bed. I told myself that someday I would be an entrepreneur so I could call my own shots, make my own way, and make my dad proud of me. I was determined to never have to beg a union rep on the phone to stop calamity from landing on my house. Dad died a few years after that. He was only fifty years old. Heart attack is what they listed on the death certificate. Broken heart was the actual cause. He never got over it. He never got to see my business either. I hope somehow, somewhere, he can see it, and I hope that he respects me for it and the work I've done.

The chime of the front door opening brings me back to myself. It's the stocky El Elegido with the deep Texas voice, and he's wearing his full club colors just as he looked the night before. Bob Culp was with him this time. "How you doing this morning, Boss?" Culp asks in a weak, almost trembling voice.

"I'm fine. How are you boys today?"

At that point, Texas takes over the discussion and Bob seems to cower as he speaks. "You Mike?"

"Yeah."

"I've got something for you," he says, thrusting a thick, beat-up envelope with a fat rubber band holding it together.

Interstate Motorcycles

Taking the bundle, I can see it is stuffed with cash, multiple denominations in no certain order. "What's this?"

"Deposit it, but don't spend it. We will be in touch with you on where it goes."

"How much is in here?" I ask while turning the bundle in my hand.

"How in the hell do I know?" Texas booms, louder than before. "Do I look like an accountant to you?" I looked at Bob but he turned his face away from me. "Just do what we ask you and we can all make some money. Okay? Let's go, little sister," he tells Bob, and they head back out the door.

"What's up with that?" Lori wants to know.

"Well," as I finish counting the bundle. "I would say it's up to 4, 651 bucks."

"What's it for?"

"He didn't say. He just said deposit it for now and they will tell us what to do with it later."

"Just hold it?" She was suspicious.

"That's what he said."

The chime notifies us of another visitor. It is Dean Macfarland from Community Commercial and he has an attractive, petite young woman with him. "Mike, Lori, how are you both? I would like to introduce my associate Joy to you."

"It is nice to meet you," the young woman very professionally says, firmly shaking hands with both of us. "So, what's up?" Dean asks.

"Well," I begin, "US Bancorp is finished with us. It was their call, not ours. You have been interested in our business for quite a while so we called you right off."

"I'm not surprised," Dean quickly answered while his pretty associate stood by nodding her head yes. "You are not the only small business we have heard from in the last couple of weeks. US Bancorps's stock is crashing and the Fed is pumping stimulus money into them as fast as they can print the bills. They are cashing out of everything in sight trying to turn their long-term assets into cash immediately to fluff up their balance sheet and hopefully save the whole corporation."

"Where does that leave small community banks like you?"

"We are stronger than ever. We are the beneficiaries of the big banks' foolishness. While they are running from businesses like yours, we are running toward them. I don't think we will have any problem handling your lines of credit and the mortgage on the property. We can take the applications right now and I will hand-walk them through. We can even open a business checking account with you today to get the process started."

"Great," I say immediately. "If you have a deposit slip with you, we can open an account with this." I hand him ten one-hundred dollar bills of El Elegido's cash.

While Lori and Joy examine our financials together and prepare our loan applications, I give Dean a guided tour of the business. We head back to the service department where Adam

Interstate Motorcycles

would normally be and I fill him in on our service manager's misfortune. "The whole place really looks good, Mike."

"Thanks, Dean. We work awfully hard at keeping it that way. It's kind of nice to hear that someone notices once in a while."

"Folks notice," Dean assures me. "Well, if Joy and Lori are finished, we will get out of your way and let you guys get back to work."

"We are all set," Joy answers from Lori's office in a high–pitched, delicate voice. "I will get the checking account open for you today. You or Lori can stop by and pick up a pad of temporary checks any time you want. I'll get them ready for you as soon as we get back. Is this your petty cash?" Dean asks, holding up the cash deposit. "You can open the new account with less if you need to keep some of this here."

"That is from a few used parts I've sold recently. I was holding it here to deposit all at once, but then I found myself without a bank."

"You have a bank now. If you don't mind, I will call Blaine at US Bancorp to let him know we will be transitioning in as your new bank and get all of your payoff information from them."

"I don't mind a bit."

"We are glad to have your business, Mike," Dean says as he shakes my hand.

"We are glad to be with you. We should have made the switch long ago."

December 15, 2009

The weather, an improvement for this time of year around here, is sunny and a bit warmer. The snow that had fallen at the beginning of the month now all melted, but it certainly isn't riding weather yet.

The switch to our new bank is coming along smoothly. Community Commercial approved all of our applications and Dean worked directly with Blaine at our former bank to make the change. It is going to take a month or so longer, but Blaine assured both me and Dean Macfarland that he would work with us during the transition, as long as we are making progress. My new business relationship with El Elegido is taking an odd turn. When we started this venture with Bob Culp and Chainsaw, they had led me to believe that they were mostly interested in my location, and a physical place from which to operate their parts business. But that is not happening. No parts are getting sold, and they aren't using the service department area they told me they were renting at all. Texas and Culp have made several more of the odd visits like the one they had made when first I seen the two of them together. They show up unannounced

Interstate Motorcycles

and come in together. Bob always keeps his mouth shut and Texas, proudly flying his full club colors, hands me an envelope full of cash for varying amounts and in various disorganized denominations. No sign of Chainsaw. The orders are the same every time: deposit the cash and don't spend it. "We will let you know what to do with it."

The whole deal is starting to creep Lori out. She doesn't like the sound of these jokers using us for cover to unload hot bike parts to begin with, but now they are throwing cash at us that they are getting from . . . We have no idea where it was coming from.

I am trying to be more practical about the revenue. By now we are just sitting on almost twenty thousand El Elegido dollars and, although they advised me not to, I have been using some of it to maintain a positive cash flow during these slow winter weeks. I figure that if they come calling for their cash before I can make it up from sales, I will make it up from our credit line. At least that saves me the interest I would have to eventually pay on the shortfall until I have to make it up to them. It is like playing with free money, at least for the short run. But, times like they are, I'll take whatever break I can make for myself.

We are having a slight bump in sales activity from the Christmas shopping season as people are out, now that it was snow free, buying accessories and gift certificates for that special motorcycle enthusiast on their list. A little bit of traffic in the showroom is better than none. That, coupled with the cash cushion we fell into and the progress on the new bank, all combine to dial back the business pressure slightly.

Sitting at my desk in the showroom, I see an all too familiar pickup truck pull in the front and then slowly drive around back to the service department entrance. It is Adam Bower. The first

69

time I saw him since his close encounter of the worst kind with a deer on the highway. "Lori, Adam and Teri are here," I tell her as I pass through her office on my way to the back.

"When did they get here?" she asks, getting up and following me.

"They just pulled in."

"You're a sight for sore eyes, Dude." I say.

"It's good to see you too," Adam responds as he exits the truck sporting two black eyes and a massive sling on his right arm.

"Looks like you finally collected that ass whipping you've had coming for so long," I crack.

With an almost pained laugh, he says, "Yeah, I guess you're right."

Teri and Lori go into Lori's office to retell the whole hospital experience, girl's style, while Adam and I go back to the service department, Adam's kingdom, so he can see what's been happening. "It's been pretty quiet," I reassure him.

"I'm not sure how long I'm going to be laid up with this arm, Mike. I . . ."

"You take as long as you need, Adam. We will make it just fine through the slow months and we will make whatever arrangements we need once the season kicks off to make sure it works out for both of us."

He knows I meant it and, looking down at the gray enamel-painted shop floor, he says, "I know we will."

Interstate Motorcycles

When Adam first came to work here, I didn't give him much of a chance, and I certainly did not give him any breaks. He had virtually no practical experience working on motorcycles. I have never been easy on young men who want to come to work for us as technicians, and Adam, with no experience and no tools, was no exception. I have always believed in the same philosophy that I had to make it in when I was a young guy working on bikes: *How bad do you want to be a motorcycle expert, punk?* I knew from very early on it wouldn't be easy, but I always wanted it bad, willing to put up with almost any amount of abuse if I could work around older guys who might be able to teach me something. Adam hit the ground on the run and exhibited two very rare qualities for a young man these days. First, he loves to work hard—the harder the better. Second, he just flat-out understands machinery, and especially motorcycles. He simply made it all look easy right from the start. Plus, as an added bonus, we liked each other pretty much right off. That is, after I stopped bitching at him relentlessly just to see if he could take it. He could and he did, without ever whining about it. I just can't bear being around whiners and sissies all day. Adam is definitely, demonstrably, neither. I respect that in a guy.

Without warning or introduction, Bob Culp is standing in the shop with us. He looks like crap, even for Bob. His mouth is swollen and his chin is bruised from one cheek to the other. I ask, "What, on earth, happened to you?"

"Oh, nothing." He is almost whimpering, looking downward with darkened eyes like a welterweight contender who just lost a title fight. "I need to talk to you, Boss."

"So, talk."

"Can we talk privately?" he says, looking hard at me in an attempt not to acknowledge Adam.

"I have to get going anyway," Adam says without hesitation, reading the moment and heading toward the shop.

"So what's up?" I ask.

"The club . . ." Culp pauses, collecting his thoughts. "The club is . . ."

"Is what?" I press him.

"I'm splitting, headed out to Florida to live with my stepmom."

Bob was always a quitter. It is in his DNA. I wasn't surprised he couldn't even make it at his lifelong dream. "Prospecting for El Elegido not what you were hoping for, huh?"

"Well". . ."

"Well! What the heck is that supposed to mean, you meatball? You got me involved with these clowns and now you are going to tell me what? Well! That's it?"

"These are bad guys, Mike. I guess I didn't realize what was going on. I just want to ride with a solid club of hardcore bikers. You know?"

Bob may have a lot of faults, but under the surface he really does just want to be a serious motorcycle enthusiast. He has just always been too stupid to separate all of this crazy color-wearing crap out from motorcycling in its purist form. "So what's up? Did they put that ass beating on you that you are wearing all over your face?"

He just looks off to the corner of the shop as if to say to me that he already felt bad enough about it without me reminding

Interstate Motorcycles

him. Besides, he at least had the testosterone to come and warn me. But warn me of what? "All right, so what's up?"

"I'm trying to quit the club."

"So quit! What's the problem?"

"It's not that easy."

"Sure it is. I just had a guy in here a couple of weeks ago who quit a club in Bakersfield. It can be done, but he had to give them his wheels."

"The stuff that these guys are involved in is heavier than any other club I've ever heard of. They don't let insiders get out."

"Hell, you're not even a full member yet. You're still a prospect. Give them back the patch; give them your motorcycle if they want it. You can be rid of them and get another one later. It's better than taking another beating from those guys, ain't it?"

"Look, I've got to go. I just wanted to stop by to tell you"—he looks directly at me—"that these guys are dangerous. I plugged you into them thinking they were really all right, so I figured I, at least, owed it to you to let you know that I was out, and I'm leaving before things get any worse for me."

Without saying another word or offering any more explanation, Bob leaves the building. Adam walks slowly back up, having overheard part of our conversation. We look at each other a little confused and, moreover, concerned. "What have you got going with these guys, Mike?"

"I'm not really sure, Adam. But I can tell you for sure I'm pulling the plug on it."

I leave Adam to survey his domain in the shop for a while. Shortly, he tells me he is headed home to take some pain meds for that busted arm and was gone. Just Lori and I are there when we have another visitor who enters the front door of the showroom with a small, frail-looking girl at his side. She is wearing a sweater large enough to fit three of her, all at the same time. The neck droops off of one shoulder down to her wrist, nearly fully exposing a large part of her not too well endowed chest. Her hair is a puffed up, brassy-colored blonde that falls in a long ponytail between her thin shoulder blades. Under the oversized knit sweater is the tiniest, virtually nonexistent remnant of a micro miniskirt that makes no real attempt at hiding the black and lace floss thong that almost covers her reproductive organs. Bottoming off the classic hooker outfit is a pair of patent leather, over-the-knee, spike-heeled dominatrix boots. The john escorting the pathetic wench is a caricature himself. He's a middle-aged Mexican fellow with jet-black hair greased straight back. His dark brown face bears a long ragged scar running the full length from his left temple down across his cheek and ending on the tip of his chin. His mouth was framed by a thin, shiny black moustache. He had an athletic build like he could be a boxer or a professional cage fighter. His trousers fit so tight that they could have been Spandex, virtually painted onto his muscular legs. Only his jacket, black leather of course, fit loosely, the better to hide bulky objects underneath. The back bore what I knew would be there without looking: El Elegido colors.

His pupils, solid black, void of any distinction from center to white, were sharp and focused. He quickly scanned the entire store and locked on me. In an almost uncharacteristically mild tone, he asks, "Are you Mike?"

Interstate Motorcycles

Without words I glance toward the business office door where Lori is standing, looking toward me for clues. I give her an almost imperceptible nod, which she recognizes as the signal to disappear back to her desk. She did without hesitation. The Mexican at the entrance catches the whole communication between us. Looking back and locking eyes with me, he says knowingly, "Mike?"

"I'm Mike."

"I am the Midwest president of El Elegido, and I think you have something that belongs to me," he says with a heavy accent.

"I have some cash that your members have been bringing by for deposit."

The girl begins slowly walking toward the jackets, looking longingly at them. She holds up a beautifully embroidered sleeve of one of the ladies jackets. "Look at this, baby?" she says in a feminine voice that sounds a little raspy, like she has a cold.

"Get your worthless little ass back in the car, bitch, before I turn you out to Mr. Mike right here on his floor!" he shouts while not taking his eyes off mine. She obediently disappears out the door and into the car on the lot. While still moving slowly toward me and not acknowledging her request or exit at all, he says, "Silly bitches. You just have to know how to talk to them. Have you been depositing the cash like we asked?"

"Yes. What happened to Chainsaw?"

"Chainsaw?" the Mexican flinches backward. "He got in a little trouble with the Feds and was bringing down more heat than he was ever worth. Just between you and me, Mr. Mike, Chainsaw was a pussy." He lets out loud, uproarious laughter.

"Was?"

"You won't be doing business with him anymore. I'm the one you will work with from here on."

"So, what do you want me to do with the money I have on deposit for you?"

"Now we are getting somewhere, Mr. Mike. The cash! That's what we're talking about. You should be sitting on a little over twenty Gs for me, Mr. Mike, and I'm here to make some—how do you say?—*disbursements*."

"That's about right."

"Here is what you are going to do: send checks to these addresses." He hands me a list of six mailing addresses. "Each check will be from your business account in the amount of three thousand dollars even. Whatever is left over is yours. They will be mailed today. If you miss this deadline, it will go very bad for you and perhaps your lovely wife as well. If you follow my instructions, we will be starting a long and profitable friendship. Are we clear?" he asks, looking toward Lori's office and smiling large, exposing his extensive gold bridgework.

"We're clear, friend."

"*Bueno,* and we are not friends yet, Mr. Mike. This is as friendly as you may ever find me. From here forward, you will not ask questions or share our business with anyone, including the pretty lady in the office, or you will have to see the unfriendly side of me. Am I getting through to you?"

"You are."

Without saying another word, the Mexican turns and put on his colors while walking slowly toward the door. He reaches out to the jacket near the front door that the young hooker admired. "Put this on my tab," he says, taking it by the hanger and carrying it out with him. The real gangsters are in town now.

Evening—December 15

The rest of the afternoon was quiet, both in terms of customers and between Lori and me. She was well aware that we had a new problem to handle, and she realized that this one was dangerous. It was no longer a matter of cash flow and paying bills. It was no longer a problem of a motorcycle club using my dealership as a front to peddle stolen motorcycle parts. We were in something far worse than hot parts and more dangerous, and I really wasn't sure what it even was. She waited patiently till after supper, when we were both alone in our home, for the explanation and the new game plan that she hoped I would have. All she knew was that I had not mailed the checks as the Mexican had instructed, and that was making her very uncomfortable.

It was not the first time we have seen trouble together. Lori and I have been together for thirty-four years, a remarkable length to stay together for two children of the 1960s, a long enough time to have seen our share of ups and downs. Always moving toward the ultimate joint objective of owning a motorcycle dealership that we could make a living in. But now we find ourselves being swallowed whole by an economic recession and by crushing financial forces that we have no control over. Things seemed a lot easier years ago.

We first met when I was racing motorcycles with a guy named Diamond Jim. I was twenty-one, and Jim and I had a pair of matching Triumph Bonnevilles. We kept them in racing condition by fixing bikes wherever we could find the work. Jim was quite a ladies' man. He always had a new groupie at his house or with him in the pits, and he was always sure that she was "the one." The guy just loved to fall in love. The problem was that there was always someone new to fall in love with.

One of Jim's girlfriends was a cute brunette named Julie. She was well educated, working on a graduate degree at Southern Illinois University, and very athletic. She played first base on a nationally ranked, traveling fast-pitch softball team. She always struck me as being out of Jim's league, a girl who was going places and not places that smelled like burning tire rubber and Klotz racing fuels. But they dated for several weeks and she seemed to genuinely like him. One Friday night before a race, Julie showed up at Jim's while he and I were in the garage finishing up the bikes and loading his van. She introduced us both to a friend of hers who she had gone to elementary school with: Lori. She knocked me out as soon as I laid eyes on her. Lori's family had moved away from the area after grade school but the two girls had stayed in touch. She was back in town and staying with Julie for the weekend and the girls were interested in coming to the race track with us. I was thrilled!

Saturday morning was just a practice day, but Jim and I used the track time well to dial in our suspension setups. It worked out. That afternoon I qualified for the main with a second place finish in my first qualifying race. Jim won the last chance qualifier later in the day, which put us both in the twenty-five-lap main event, which had a thousand-dollar purse paid out to the top five finishers. Putting a thousand bucks on the table at a regional semi-pro flat-track motorcycle race was like tossing a whole frozen chicken into a pit full of alligators. All of the riders were hungry.

My lap time had placed me on the inside rail of the third row. Not bad. Jim was somewhere behind me and I only hoped that he wouldn't take me out with one of those crazy inside-out, turn-one-hole shots that he was known for when he was deep in the grid. He usually started ahead of me and I always tried to tuck in behind him on that move so when we got to the apex of the first turn he would clear a path in front of me like the Red Sea in front of Moses and the Israelites. This time, I was just part of the traffic he would be looking to crowd wide. Getting through the first turn well is critical. Twenty-five motorcycles, piloted by speed junkies with heavy throttle hands, all converging on a single spot at the apex of the turn, and all trying to be there first, is a design for a serious crash. As I slid the bike wide to the outside rail, exiting the turn onto the back straight, I knew I had started well but did not know how many bikes were in the now forming single-file line of bikes accelerating in front of me. The green flag was still showing as the group I was behind cocked the bikes to the side, throwing them into turn three at the end of the straight. One, two, three, four bikes turned in before me. That put me in fifth place, a money position. I tucked and pinned the throttle, following the leaders down the front straight, completing lap one wondering where Diamond Jim was.

At lap thirteen, the starter in the tower showed the crossed flags, indicating the race was at the halfway point. I was still in fifth and now had a line on the turns that had me back in touch with the four hotdogs in front. But, where was Jim? Several bikes were stopped, off the racing line and out of the hunt, with mechanical failures. There still had been no yellow flags,

Interstate Motorcycles

meaning that we had run half of a dash-for-cash main event without a crash. Unheard of!

As we came under the flag tower on the front straight to start lap twenty-two, I was in a three-way drag race with a Harley XR on my outside and a Triumph Bonneville on my inside. It was Jim, and he was all out for a money finish now.

The three of us fanned into turn one, Jim took me on the inside line for fifth and the XR fading behind me. As Jim and I exited turn two virtually side by side, Jim took me wide to the guard rail, and while he and I were bumping and grinding for fifth, the XR squared off the turn and beat both of us onto the back straight. One hundred ten miles an hour, one twenty, one twenty-five. I held the throttle on, none of the three of us wanting to be the first to slam the throttle off and toss the bike in. At the very last microsecond before overcooking into the hay bales, all three of us turned in at the same time. Jim bumped the XR, I bumped Jim, the XR's rear wheel clipped my front, I drifted up and wacked Jim's left handlebar. None of us crashed, back on the front straight, back in the tuck, back on the throttle. One hundred fifteen, one hundred twenty-five, a buck thirty, turn one was coming fast and no one was letting up. I wondered if I could make this turn this fast.

Remarkably, the fierce racing for fifth place had the three of us right on top of the group of four bikes that had led the thing, swapping spots with each other from the start. Ending lap twenty-four, the starter's tower furiously waved the solid white flag marking the beginning of the final lap. Seven bikes bunched tightly together, waging war for the top five paying positions. As we passed under the tower, I was running seventh and easing by the XR on the inside, well in position to beat him to the back straight in sixth place, with Diamond Jim dead ahead of me and driving hard. As we grinded it out at over one hundred thirty down the back straight for the last time today,

I was easing up on Jim's inside and well placed to take him wide and out of the money on turn three. No hard feelings. He would have done it to me. We were handlebar-to-handlebar as we both squared up and tossed the bikes in at three, me inside and him out, knowing all the while we had a hot XR right behind us somewhere. As we stuffed them in, the bike just feet ahead of us in fourth made hard contact with the bike ahead of him in third. The impact momentarily straightened up both of them as we rounded turn four, the last turn of the race. Neither of them crashed out, but having to get out of the throttle to save the ride on the way up to the front straight away set up a four-wide, side-by-side drag race in hot pursuit of the last three paid places. Jim and I had the hole shot onto the last pass under the tower, still locked along side of each other as if welded together. The two bikes we squeezed past in the final turn had a little more engine than either of us and, given a long enough run, they would surely get around. At one hundred thirty-five miles an hour, it seemed like a lifetime to get to the flagman, now down on the track surface, leaping and waving the much coveted and long fought for black and white checkered flag.

In the tightest photo finish ever recorded at the old half-mile oval raceway, I ended up with third and my teammate and old friend a whisker behind me at the line in fourth. Both in the money!

The few spectators in the stands that night were all on their feet screaming, shouting, and applauding wildly their appreciation for the great race they had just witnessed. Jim and I rounded the gate at pit in, slowly riding the bikes back to our pit area through the converging, cheering crowd, with smiles busting through our race helmets. And there was Lori. She was running toward me, laughing, crying, clapping, and dancing. "That was great," she told me as I pulled off the helmet.

Interstate Motorcycles

We kissed. I was still sitting on the bike and we kissed so hard, it nearly fell over on her. The spectators around us sent up another round of applause at the sight. We could have been on another planet for all that either of us cared—we just kept kissing. It was the sweetest-tasting kiss of my life. We married six months later and have been together ever since.

Seems like right from the beginning we were on rocky financial footing. I was already hooked on motorcycle racing, although at twenty-one I was one of the older guys, and she loved the sport from the moment the green flag waved at our first race together. Lori learned early on that I hoped I could actually make it as a pro, and she encouraged me to try. She figured out the politics of the pits after just a few races. She knew that I wasn't getting any younger and that the guys the big money teams were hiring were all teenagers, and fearless. The only shot we had was to make a lot of races, and win, in hopes of attracting the attention of a factory team. So I managed to make a deal on a Chevy van with a hundred thousand miles on it that would serve as our transportation, race-prep trailer, and living quarters the first summer we were together, and we mapped out a course through the Midwest, hitting race tracks and fairgrounds in search of victories and prize money to sustain us. As romantic as it sounded, we were miserable. The bike broke, a lot. The van broke, a lot. We were only eating once a day, and that was mostly peanut butter sandwiches. The coveted wins and prize money were sparse. The final straw was at a Kansas county fair race in early August that paid a thousand dollars split among the top three finishers. We arrived there and spent the last of our money on entry fees and fuel, both of us knowing that if I didn't win something we were going to be as broke as our equipment. "You got a plan?" she asked me with hopeful eyes while I put on my leathers.

"I'll just have to win," I told her with a smile and an enthusiastic tone.

The bike ran well in practice and I had some pretty good tires to put on for qualifying that I hoped would last through the main event. I pulled a good starting position on the second row for my heat race, but when the green flag dropped I felt like I had the weight of the world on that bike with me. Three laps into the heat, I was stuck in the middle of a fast field and pushing hard to get up front when I lost traction on the front wheel trying to pass on the outside and crashed the Bonneville hard into the hay bales. It was bent up pretty good and I had a broken left forearm.

It was the first time I felt responsible for making Lori cry. We had no money and no health insurance but the broken arm was not dislocated so the emergency room physician put it in a splint and told me to get it checked out further when I got home. He didn't want to waste his time on a deadbeat, broke-down motorcycle racer, and I didn't blame him. Another race team that I had gotten to know on the circuit offered to buy the bent up Bonneville from me and I accepted the meager offer, graciously. They were buying it more to help us out than out of any need for the machine. That ended my pro racing season—and career.

We left the track with a full tank of gas in the van thanks to the race organizers, a couple of hundred bucks proceeds from the crashed bike, a promissory note to pay the hospital when we could, and each other. It was the first time we were ever in debt. All in all though, I felt pretty lucky.

Once we got home I found a full-time job repairing motorcycles in the area's Honda dealership. The owners of the shop and I got along well and I worked there for the next ten years as a technician, service manager, and eventually the store's general manager. Lori got an administrative job for the school district and ended up working there for the next twenty years. We paid the hospital bill in full, but I never got

Interstate Motorcycles

a follow-up on the arm. It healed fine on its own even though it's a bit crooked to this day. We found a church we fit into pretty well and became regulars. I felt a strong connection to God through those years and came to really believe that he would protect Lori and me and allow us to prosper. We bought a little house and were saving some money. We found out early in our marriage that Lori was unable to bear children, which saddened us both greatly, but still they were good years.

When the Honda shop's owners decided to retire, they closed up the store and I was, for the first time in a decade, unemployed. Lori and I decided to roll the dice again so we opened Interstate Motorcycles. I was finally an *entrepreneur,* and I hoped my dad would be proud.

The store did pretty well. I had a lot of contacts in the industry from my years in the Honda shop and a lot of good customers as well. Some years revenues were up, and some years they were down. But overall I managed to make a living, and when Lori had the opportunity to take an early retirement from the school district she joined me full time at the shop. It's been exhilarating. Not quite as dangerous as two twenty-year-old kids rambling around trying to make a living racing motorcycles, but risky and rewarding nevertheless. The rewards have been lacking in recent years however. The global recession has extracted a lethal toll on our small community, and our business. The many factories that used to pepper the area with decent-paying full-time jobs have all folded up or moved away, leaving most of our regular customers unemployed. When money is tight, motorcycles become an unaffordable luxury, not a necessity, and that has put our sales in a tailspin. Our backs are against the wall: too young and too deep in debt to retire and running out of resources to borrow from to keep the place open. We are entering the winter months when we know things will slow down even further, and now we are in

85

bed with an outlaw motorcycle club funneling cash through us for God only knows what.

"So," Lori began the conversation, "have you got a plan?"

"I'm going to call the cops tomorrow and turn the whole thing over to them."

"You heard the Mexican: don't talk to anyone," her voice trembled a little.

"Lori, I don't care what the Mexican said. I'm turning this whole thing over to the authorities."

She didn't answer but looked hard at me. I think she was hoping for some reassurance that the police would be able to take care of it. "It's going to be fine," I said, gently taking her by the hand. "I have always taken good care of those boys' motorcycles over at the sheriff's office. They know us, and I'm going to let them handle this whole deal. Look, I'm thinking maybe you should head down to Florida to visit your sister for Christmas, till I can root these clowns out of our business and out of our lives."

"I can't do that."

"Sure you can. You have wanted to see her for months. Business is slow. I can handle the shop solo for a couple of weeks. I'll meet you down there right after Christmas and we can spend New Year's there together on winter hiatus. We will just close the shop for a week or two."

"No! I'll be worried sick about you up here handling all of this by yourself."

Interstate Motorcycles

"I won't be handling all of this by myself. I won't be handling it at all. I told you, I'm turning it over to the sheriff."

"Well, then why are you trying to hide me? You know it won't be that easy."

"I just want you to be out of this, right now. Those guys know that they can get to me easier by threatening you. With you out of their reach, it will be easier for me to get rid of them. Believe me, it will be a faster, cleaner break with you out of reach."

"Mike, I don't want to leave. I don't want to be away from you with these crazies in our business." We hug and gently kiss. Still the sweetest taste my lips will ever touch, still after all of these years. As we hold each other at the foot of our bed, there is both a sense of strength and of ongoing dread. Dread not only over El Elegido, but over the many things that are adversely affecting us that we cannot make go away. "Tell me we will be okay," She says.

"We will be okay."

We kiss, lie down. I slowly undress her. She is beautiful.

December 16, 2009

The morning starts out cloudy and overcast, a gloomy reminder of winter. No motorcycle ride to work this morning—too cold and icy. Driving my pickup truck to work is decidedly not as interesting, so I fumble around with the radio trying to find a weather report calling for clearing skies and warmer air. No such luck. The crackling signal from the local rock and roll station is about all I can get.

"Good morning, Missouri. This is Woody Wheeler coming at you from KXLN FM, your home for the hottest rock and roll in the central Missouri Ozarks. We have to interrupt this morning's drive-time tunes to bring you breaking news. A disturbing report on US highway 63 north between Rolla and Vichy, Missouri, has the highway shut down in both directions because of a body found laying on the road in the traffic lanes. We have Jerod Brown, KXLN's afternoon show host, live from the grizzly scene. Jerod, are you there?"

"Yeah, I'm on with you, Woody."

Interstate Motorcycles

"So, there is a body, a human body on the road up there? What's going on?"

"Right, a human being's body is up here on the road, Woody. The scene is truly surreal. I actually have Tyrell Gill with me now, and he was one of the first witnesses here to call police and report the find. Just to give our listeners a heads up, Highway 63 is completely closed in both directions and cordoned off with crime-scene tape and authorities are strongly advising motorists who normally use this corridor to find and use an alternative route. So, Tyrell, what can you tell us about what you seen here this morning?"

"Well, I was on my way home from the Walmart distribution center where I work the third shift. As I came up on the body in the dark, I thought it was a deer at first. So I slowed down as I got up on it and then I could see it. I could actually see the bottoms of bare feet pointing back at me. I pulled right over and fixed my headlights on him and ran out to see if I could help. I was thinking then that it was maybe someone who got hit crossing the highway or something, but there wasn't any other traffic around right then."

"What did you see when you got up to the body, Tyrell?"

"Well," he says, pausing to swallow hard and take a deep breath, "there was a barefooted guy laying there on the centerline, in tore-up old blue jeans and no shirt, just a ragged-looking vest. The back of the vest was all chopped up, like with a razor knife. His hands were behind his back and were wired tight together at the wrist with a piece of barbed fence wire, and". . ." He again swallows hard. "There was no head. I never seen nothing like it before! It didn't have any head."

"Tyrell, I hate to cut you off, but that officer over there is signaling for you. Looks like he wants you over there by his car, maybe?

"I have to go."

"You going to be all right, Tyrell? Well, he's gone over to the police cruiser, Woody. It is hard to believe. That's about all we've got from the scene right now. The authorities here are waving for us to get back. The state police and sheriff's office are here in force searching the area. Again, they have this highway completely shut down and want us to pass along to our listeners that this area may be closed for a while. No one is getting through so if you were driving this way, find another route. Woody, back to you."

"Thanks, Jerod. It sounds crazy up there. Things like that just don't happen around here. Keep us posted if you hear anything else. And, of course, we will keep all of you posted. But now back to the hottest rock and roll in the Missouri Ozarks. It is 6:27 a.m. and you're listening to KXLN."

"Hmm," I say to the dashboard radio as if it can answer me. "I wonder what that's about."

It is always more difficult to open the shop on days like this when you can be pretty certain that business will be slow, or even nonexistent. It seems to take more effort.

Lori stayed at home on the phone, checking flights and costs for the trip to Pensacola. She's going. It's the best thing. She still seems to think she should be here, but I've been able to convince her that I can handle it more effectively, with the aid of the sheriff's department, with her safely out of the way. I call the sheriff's office. Deputy Tom Hughes, a young guy and local boy, and a Harley-Davidson owner who I knew fairly

Interstate Motorcycles

well, answers the phone. "Good morning, Tom. This is Mike Douglas at Interstate Motorcycles."

"Hey, Mike, how you doing on a cold December morning in the Ozarks?"

"Good. Listen, I wonder if you guys could have someone stop by sometime today. I've got a little situation I need to talk to you about."

"Is it an emergency?"

"No, not really, any time today someone can make it by will be fine. I seem to be having a little trouble with a new motorcycle club in town."

"We will get someone over today, Mike. I'm not sure what time it will be. We have everyone up north of town on US 63 working the crime scene."

"Yeah, I heard the story on the radio this morning. Someone get their head knocked off, run over by a truck or something?"

"That's not what I'm hearing. Anyway, I've got to go, Mike. We'll get someone out to see you sometime today."

"All right, Tom, I appreciate it."

Poor wretch. Probably a walker on the shoulder, run over by a hit-and-run drunk driver. I hope they find the guy and throw the book at him.

The front door chime sounds, signaling today's first customer. It's Tim Walker and he's actually an old friend. "How you doing today, Mike?" he asks with his classic Arkansas twang. "Hey, look here, man. I want to get some prices on a pair of tires for my old Harley. Figured now would be a good time to get 'em cause you could use the business this time of year, and I'd be ready to ride first thing next spring."

"I appreciate that, Tim. How 'bout a cup of coffee?"

"Well, that sounds real good."

Tim is a fairly young guy, probably forty-five although he looks older than his years—looks like going on sixty. He's about fifty pounds overweight, mostly around the gut, but strong in his chest, arms, and legs, the result of being a construction worker his whole life. His eyes always seem to be smiling, exaggerating the deep wrinkles in his dark-tanned, leathery skin. Tim and I have been friends since the first time he brought his bike to us for work. An unlikely friendship though, since Tim is a dyed-in-the-wool Harley-Davidson rider who has flown the colors of several of the areas more notorious clubs, and I have always been better known as a sport bike type and former motorcycle racer. The guy's a real motorcycle enthusiast though, as am I. He has pretty well separated himself from the motorcycle club scene lately, following a drug distribution charge that landed him in the penitentiary a couple of years ago. But he stays in touch with the scene. While he poured himself a cup of coffee, it occurred to me to ask him about El Elegido. "Looks like there's a new club in town," I mention casually.

Tim's smiling eyes turn stern and serious as he stops pouring and snaps his head around to face me. "Who might that be, Mike?"

"A group with a Spanish name: El Elegido."

"What do you know about them?"

Interstate Motorcycles

"I've just seen them around. What do you know about them?"

"Have they been coming in here?"

"Yeah, a few times."

Tim's eyes lower to the floor as he sips the Styrofoam cup. "Have they asked you to do any business with them?"

"As a matter of fact, they have. I've been holding some cash for them."

His head pops back up to lock eyes with me. "You need to get rid of those guys as fast as you can, Mike. They are dope dealers, gun runners, and killers."

"Killers?"

"Everywhere those guys go they leave a path of dead bodies behind them. They're no good, and I'm surprised you would have let them get a hold on you."

"They made me an offer I didn't think I could refuse, at the time. I called the sheriff's office this morning. I'm letting them handle it, but.". . ."

"But?"

"Well, I spent some of the money they brought in. Just what was supposed to be my rent payment for the use of the service department at night."

After a short pause, Tim asks, "Are you serious? You spent some of it already? Mike, that is going to make you an accessory to drug dealing, especially when you mention the name of the

93

gang. Believe me: the authorities are after these guys. You hand this off to the sheriff, and they are likely to lock you up on the spot and keep you in for a while. And, if what I know about these guys holds true, they'll kill you on the inside. They have plenty of convicts willing to shank a guy for them, from county lockups to federal pens. You got yourself a whole house full of trouble here.

"Look," Tim goes on, putting down his coffee and reaching for the business cards in his wallet. "I wouldn't tell the cops anything yet if I were you. I know a bounty hunter I met about something else while I was doing time. He's been up here from New Mexico sniffing around for these guys. He's some kind of a former special forces operator or something. I ran into him at the bar two nights ago and he was asking about El Elegido. "Crap," he says, still rummaging around in his wallet. "I don't have that card with me. Let me run to the house and find it. He's a serious player, Mike, and he's got a serious beef with this outfit. I'm not sure of the details why, but I do know that if I was in your shoes, I'd want him on my side."

"Thanks for the info, Tim."

"If it was anyone else, I wouldn't have anything to do with this, bro, but I can't leave you twisting in the wind. You armed?"

"Yeah."

"Good! Be careful. You're on thin ice here, and, whatever you do, keep Lori out of here."

"I will. She is making flight reservations to Florida right now."

"Let me go find that number. I'll get right back with you."

Interstate Motorcycles

"Thanks again, Tim. Oh, by the way," I ask as he quickly heads for the door, "what's the guy's name?"

"Muntze. His name is Muntze. I've got to move. You watch yourself."

Tim beats it out of there as if he thought he might get caught in a crossfire. As he is driving off, Lori calls. "I can get on an Air Tran flight out of St. Louis to Houston, Texas, with a connecting commuter flight to Pensacola for only one hundred forty-nine dollars," she tells me. "Then if you are driving down for New Year's, I will just ride home with you."

"What's not to love about that?"

"Well, the problem is to get that price. The flight is tomorrow morning."

"Make the reservation before it's fully booked. Use the company credit card."

"You think I should?"

"Yes! It's the perfect deal. Just go ahead and lock it in."

"But I don't have anything ready."

"Go to church and take care of your business there, then go home and get packed. I'm telling you it's the perfect deal. You should jump on this, Lori."

"Are you sure you want to do this?"

At that moment, she had no idea how much I was sure. As calmly and as thoughtfully as I can, I say, "Yes, I really want to get out of town. I will meet you down there in a couple of weeks."

"All right." I can hear her smiling on the other end of the line. "It does sound like fun."

"It will be, Lori. I'm looking forward to it already."

A couple of hours and several shoppers after talking to Lori, a marked sheriff's deputy car pulls onto the lot and two plain-clothes deputies get out. They enter the building with their heads on a swivel. Their body language and demeanor clearly mark these guys as law-enforcement officers. One is a really fat, baldheaded guy wearing a long gray, rumbled overcoat. The other guy is also on the heavy side but younger. He is wearing a suit and jacket but no tie. I figure he was probably the apprentice for the fat guy. Looking down at a pocket-sized, spiral-bound notebook flipped open in his palm, the younger guy asks, "Mr. Douglas?"

"That's me." I reached out to shake their hands. "I'm Mike Douglas."

"I'm Detective Peterson. This is my partner, Detective Robb. We understand you placed a call about"—he looks back down at his notebook—"a motorcycle club?"

"Yes, sir, that's right."

"What seems to be the problem, Mike?" the younger guy, Peterson continued.

I compose myself as best I can, noticing that these two are examining my every move as carefully as they would a suspect. "Well, fellows, I've been visited by a club that, I guess is new in town. I've never seen them before. They come in here mostly

Interstate Motorcycles

belligerent and generally intimidate other customers. They show up three or four at a time, and spread out all over the building so I can never keep an eye on all of them at once. They never buy anything, but remarkably we keep coming up short on merchandise after they leave."

The two of them are staring, expressionless, at me. The fat guy's jaw is hanging open and his fat baggie eyes sag like he needs some sleep, giving him kind of a basset hound look. Peterson asks, "Do you know the name of this club, Mr. Douglas?"

"El Elegido is what the patch on their jackets say."

"El Elegido? Is that Spanish," Peterson asks, looking over at the basset hound. Detective Robb neither acknowledges his partner's question nor that he has even addressed him for that matter. "Is that Spanish?" Peterson throws the question at me.

"Yes, I think it means 'The Chosen," I respond.

"Hmm, *The Chosen*," Peterson says, writing it in his notes.

"Do you know someone named Bob Culp?" the fat guy asks me out of the clear blue with a mouth full of slobber.

"Yeah, I know him."

"Does he work here?" Peterson speaks up again.

"No. He did about a year ago, but no more."

"Did you have a falling out?"

"Not really. He was just a lousy mechanic. Why do you ask?"

"Well, Mr. Douglas, Bob Culp was found dead this morning."

"Dead? What happened to him?"

"Well, we were hoping you could help us to figure that out, Mr. Douglas." Peterson was asking all of the questions now while Robb waddled to the side and leaned hard against the handlebars of the Guzzi California Vintage. "Do you know if he was affiliated in any way with this gang, El Elegido?"

I am quite sure by the tone of the question that he knows very well that Culp was part of the club. "Yes, he is."

"Was he ever in here while this club was around, intimidating your customers and pilfering your merchandise?"

"Yes, he was. Can I ask what happened to Bob?"

"Oh, I'm sorry. Didn't I mention that? He was found lying on US Highway 63 just north of here this morning." They both study my reaction to the news carefully.

"The guy with no head?" I ask, genuinely stunned.

"So you heard?"

"Well, it's all over the radio. Tom Hughes even told me about it when I called your office this morning."

"Tom Hughes, huh?" Robb chimes in, writing Tom's name on a little yellow piece of paper he whips out of the inside pocket of his coat.

"Anybody you know want to do anything to hurt Bob Culp that you can think of, Mike?"

"No. Bob was a drunk, but he never hurt anybody that I know of."

"I see. Have you seen this *club* recently?"

"One of them was here yesterday."

"Culp?"

"No, a Mexican guy who I've never seen before. Bob wasn't with him."

They both were scribbling notes. "Did you get a name of this Mexican guy?" Peterson asks.

"No."

"What did he want?"

The moment of truth has just arrived. Do I tell him about the money? Or do I hold out to hear from Walker? I'm trusting my old friend Walker over these two for now. "He was just shopping."

"Anything missing?"

"Not that I've been able to find so far."

"Was it the visit from this Mexican guy that somehow convinced you to call us?"

"Not really. It was more the cumulative effect of these jokers coming in and out of here."

"I see." We all pause. They check their notes and continuing to watch me while I check my emotions and watch them back. "Is there anything else you want to tell us about, Mr. Douglas?"

He seems to be teeing me up to tell him something. "No, that's it. I just thought the sheriff's department should be made aware of these guys. They look like trouble."

"We appreciate that, Mike. We think they're trouble too and we want to get some answers from them. Listen, you can level with me here, and now is the best time for you to do it. Are you a prospect for this club?"

"No, I am not. Why would I be calling you to complain about a club that I was a part of?"

"We just have to ask Mike," Peterson says, handing me his business card. "If anything else comes up or comes to mind, give me a call directly. My personal number is right here. You have a very nice store here, sir."

It was a peculiar visit. I started out trying to be an honest citizen, and ended up looking more like a suspect in a murder case. Walker was right. If I had told to these guys about the money laundering, I'd be on my way to the county lockup, at least for further interrogation. El Elegido killed Bob Culp. Looks like he was right too. He knew he needed to get out of town fast to get clear of these guys. I hope that his taking the extra time to warn me didn't delay him long enough to get him killed. Culp was a loser but he never deserved that. "My God, have mercy. They cut off his head? My God, what is happening here?

Thinking about it makes for a long afternoon. It's nearly six o'clock in the evening before Walker calls. "Mike, I got a hold of Muntze. He wants to know if you can meet him at the Twisty Road Bar tonight after you shut down."

"I'm about to close up now. What time does he want to meet?"

"Well, we are both here now having a beer."

"I'll be there in thirty minutes."

The Twisty Road is a biker bar where most of the clubs hang out. It's located well out of town on a paved county highway just called Z. It's far enough away from other neighbors for all hell to break loose about every night, and it usually does. I know lots of the guys who are regulars there, but I make it a point to avoid the place. More drama than I want. There are only a couple of cars on the parking lot when I get there and, even though the temperature is now a few degrees below freezing, there are two older model Harleys out front with massively high *ape hanger* handlebars. As I push open the old wooden door, which is desperate for paint, the hinges let out a high-pitched squeak that alerts the few customers in the dimly lit bar to swivel around and see who is coming in. When the door slaps closed against the jamb behind me, I nod to all of the people who are looking me over. Just a couple of heads nod back, and then everyone gets back to their drinks and discussions. It's a small, elongated floor plan with a bar along the length of the back wall and mismatched tables and chairs scattered along the other. Two doors at the far end of the hallway-shaped establishment are marked "Dudes," and the other "Chicks," with a bumper pool table in front of them. I slowly walked toward a customer at the bar named Billy who I recognized. He's a regular customer of ours. "Hey, Mike, can I buy you a beer?"

"No, thanks, Billy. I'm looking for Tim Walker. You seen him?" I ask, squinting around the dark corners.

"He just left. Said he would be right back though. Why don't you have a beer?"

"He didn't say how long?"

"No, but he did say he would be right back."

The bartender is standing in front of us, eyes squeezed tightly and massaging her forehead like she has a headache. "Let me have a High Life," I say. She turns and goes for the beer without opening her eyes.

A guy from the corner near the Chicks door gets up and walks toward me; he doesn't look like a regular. About six foot tall and slender, wearing neat, dark-colored dress slacks and a white golf shirt with "PING" embroidered on the left chest. "Are you Mike?" he asks, looking over the top of what appear to be tinted prescription glasses.

"Yeah, Mike Douglas."

"I'm Greg Muntze," he answers with a friendly smile full of perfect teeth. The bartender brings back a cold bottle of beer for me and says, "Two bucks."

"Thanks." I throw her a five. "Can I buy you a beer, Mr. Muntze?"

"Just water for me," he says handing an empty glass back to her.

"Arghh," she groans, picking up the glass and the bill.

Interstate Motorcycles

"So, Walker says we need to talk. He tells me we may be able to help each other out," Muntze begins.

"Excuse us, Billy." I say. "We have some business to talk about. Let's find a table over here," I say to Muntze looking around for a spot.

"No problem, Mike," Billy says. "Good seeing you."

We sit down together at a small round cocktail table as far away from the bar's few other patrons as we can get. "Walker says you have a problem," Muntze says. His high cheek bones and chiseled facial features turn serious.

"It looks that way. Look," I whisper, leaning over the shaky table toward him, "if you don't mind my asking, what's your interest in my problem anyway?"

"Right to the point, I don't mind that at all. I prefer it. To start with, while we are here, don't use the name of the club. We will just call it your problem. You can't be sure who's listening in here. Second, I'm a bail bondsman and fugitive recovery agent licensed in New Mexico." He shows me an official-looking photo ID badge.

"So, you're a bounty hunter."

"If you prefer," Muntze says, putting the badge back in his pocket. "Anyway, the reason for my interest in your problem should be obvious. I was looking for a jumper who was running with them."

"Was? Did you already get him?"

"No. He's dead. I didn't pinch him soon enough. But I recovered the corpse, so I'm off the hook for the bond."

"Was it Bob Culp that you were after?"

"No. It was a guy that went by Chainsaw. You might have met him."

"Yeah, I did," I reply, shaking my head. "There sure are a lot of dead bodies around my problem."

Walker comes into the bar through the squeaky front door, surveys the floor, and comes to our table. "Good, you all found each other I see. I had to run over to a bro's house real quick. He crashed his chopper and broke his foot. He wanted me to pick up some weed for him, which I told him I could not do. What was he thinking? I'm still on parole. Anyway he sent another guy to get it. The guy is meeting El Elegido here in a few minutes to score the dope. I thought you both all ought to know. "Mike," Walker says, leaning down to look at me, "I'm done with this deal from here on out. I've done all I can do for you. You're in good hands with this guy." He gestures with his thumb toward Muntze. "Do the smart thing. Give him what he wants. I'll see you around."

"Thanks, Tim," I tell him as I shake his hand. "I appreciate it." Tim Walker pivots and heads back out of the place. He doesn't need or want any trouble. "Your jumper is dead, your investment is secured, so why aren't you on your way back to New Mexico already?" I ask. "What do you want, Mr. Muntze?"

"Right now what I want is to get away from here before your problem shows up."

We exit to the cold, dark parking lot. "Where do you want to go," I ask. "We need to talk."

"We do need to talk, Mike. What time do you open your shop in the morning?"

"I'll be open for business by 9:00 a.m."

"I will be there at 9:00."

"All right, I've got to get home anyway. My wife is flying to Florida tomorrow."

"It's smart to get her out of here for awhile. In the meantime, be careful. I'll talk to you in the morning."

At home, Lori is busy getting ready for her trip. Her bag is already packed and she had lists prepared for me so that I could take care of the house to her satisfaction in her absence. She has always been big on making notes for herself. Every task listed, itemized, prioritized, and checked off one by one till the mission gets accomplished.

"I guess you booked your flight?" I ask her coming through the door that evening and noticing that "Air Tran" had a checkmark next to it on her notepad.

"Are you sure I should go? I feel like I'm bailing out on you or something. Did you talk to the sheriff's department?"

"Yes, I did."

"So what did they say?"

"They told me that they were cracking down on El Elegido already and that they were glad I contacted them."

"Are they going to lock them up, or what?"

"Yes, they are. They may have them all in custody already," I told her.

"Good. Hey, did you hear about the guy on Highway 63 this morning?"

"Yes, I did."

"It's unbelievable. I wonder what happened to him."

"Probably a meth head rambling around the highway in the middle of the night that got hit by a truck or something. Who knows?" The news had not yet released Culp's name as the headless victim, and I sure am not going to tell her now. She would connect the murder to El Elegido and it would scare her into thinking she shouldn't leave so that she can stay here and help. The biggest help she can be right now is to get to a safe place. Worrying about what might happen to her here only complicates an already complicated enough issue.

DECEMBER 17, 2009

THURSDAY MORNING AND THE weather is better: slightly warmer and mostly clear skies. The wind is light, holding out the promise of a smooth flight out of town for Lori. We finalize our plans for me to drive down after Christmas and meet her at her sister's house in Pensacola. Her mood is lighter than it has been recently. The prospect of taking a little time off from the work at the shop and heading south to warmer climates, combined with visiting her favorite sister, is having a positive impact on her. She also feels better about turning over El Elegido and their crooked cash to the authorities. I'm not sure it's a lie if I just don't correct her misconception. We kiss, hold each other for a long time, and say good-bye. I'll miss her, but I'm relieved to know she will be out of harm's way.

As I finish moving things around the showroom and turning the thermostat up to warm the place for today's work, the chime on my cell phone sounds, signaling that I have received a text message. It's from Lori: "Have cleared airport security and am waiting at the gate to board. Will call you when I get to Florida. Love you."

At 9:00 a.m. sharp, a black Acura sedan with tinted glass drives into a parking place near the front door and out jumps Greg Muntze. This is the first time I get a look at him in the light, and he definitely is not what I would think a bail bondsman and fugitive recovery agent would look like. Today he is wearing a tartan-patterned flat cap and dark-tinted aviator glasses. His head scans from left to right smoothly as he walks toward the door. He wipes the Italian-styled loafers on the floor mat and unzips the London Fog jacket as he enters looking more like he's going to a *Gentleman's Quarterly* photo shoot than a motorcycle shop. "Morning, Mike."

"Good morning, Mr. Muntze. You are right on time."

"Did your wife get out of town yet?"

"Yes, she just sent me a text that she is about to board her flight."

"Good, that's the best thing. Mike, let me get right to the point here. Listen, the money these guys have been giving you doesn't really belong to them at all. El Elegido is the retail drug sales division for some pretty serious bad guys."

"Mafia?"

"Bigger! The guy that El Elegido works for is the head of a major Mexican drug cartel. We are talking about perhaps the largest drug cartel in the world. One that is effectively waging war with the legitimate government of Mexico, and by many accounts, is winning and keeping the United States awash in a sea of illegal drugs. They have also infiltrated and are heavily connected to the top levels of business and governments on both sides of the border."

"So where do you fit in, Greg? Did one of these *top level* guys jump bail somewhere?" Who is he trying to kid?

Smiling, he says, "No. I'm not after the top guys. My interest is in your buddies, El Elegido."

"They aren't my buddies."

"You don't even know how right you are. These guys seriously intend to hurt you, and your family."

"I've got that figured out. I know what they have in mind for me, and I know that the sheriff's department has me made as an accomplice to their drug activities, which technically I guess I am. I know that at this point I'm stuck right between the two and, either way I turn, I lose. I got it! What I want to know is what you want. Walker is a friend of mine, and he says I'm going to need you. What I want you to tell me, straight up, is what do I need you for?"

Removing the dark glasses and studying me for a reaction, he says, "I can get rid of El Elegido for you." He opens the London Fog to reveal a shoulder-holstered automatic pistol.

"So you're going to kill them? Is that what you're trying to tell me?"

"It's the only way."

"And, why would you do that? I thought you were a bail bondsman?"

"Some guys just have a good killing coming."

"So kill them! What's keeping you? You need me to help you? Is that what you want from me?"

"No. You should stay out of the way. What I want from you is their money."

"Their money! Are you serious? What money? The dope money? Okay, let me say this back to you and see if I got it right. I just hand you their cash, that you say belongs to a Mexican drug cartel, and you will kill these guys before they can kill me and before the sheriff's department locks me up for being an accomplice to drug dealing and murder. Do I have it right?"

"I know, it sounds crazy," Muntze says.

"Mr. Muntze." I cut him off with a sigh. "That doesn't sound crazy; that *would be* crazy. I have my hands full enough as it is, man. The last thing I need is to get involved with another player who comes to me soliciting a contract for murder. Please". . ." I say as I again sigh heavily, "no hard feelings, but please get the hell out of here."

"You misunderstand, Mike. I'm not soliciting a contract for murder. I'm offering you my services as a bodyguard, and you're going to need it. The only reason I mention killing members of El Elegido is because I'm sure a couple of those jokers will have to go down to keep them from killing you.

"While following these guys up from New Mexico tracking my jumper, I got a good look at what they are up to. They are a bad bunch and they are raping my country. The country I served as a special forces operator all over the world for twenty years. Mike, I'm in perfect position here to break up their little party, before you or anyone else gets killed."

Interstate Motorcycles

"Why don't you just join forces with the cops?" I ask. "I'll give them the money. They are swarming around these guys right now. Let them know what you've got and let them clean these guys out."

"I already tried it," Muntze answers quickly. "While they were in Oklahoma, I tried to make a move on my guy, Chainsaw. Since I'm licensed as a fugitive recovery agent in another state, I had to notify local law enforcement before I could grab him. El Elegido was working a small business just outside of Tulsa the same way they are working you. It's a small liquor store in a Latino neighborhood.

"I figured out what they were doing is packing dope up from Mexico and selling it on the street. If they run into any resistance from the locals, selling their own dope, they just blow their heads off. They funnel the cash into an outfit the size of yours with limited resources and then squeeze the store owner to send their own company checks to legitimate mail-order gun stores around the country. The checks cover the payment on orders that have already been placed, I presume from Mexico, on military-style weapons that can be readily modified for full automatic fire. Once the payments clear, the weapons are picked up by special courier for delivery back to the purchaser who officially is the store owner who wrote the checks for the purchase. Only the weapons never make it back to the purchasers. The couriers are always Mexican contractors. Smooth, huh?

"But all good things must come to an end. Once they set up a few successful weapons purchases, the business owner becomes obsolete. Eventually, you are going to spark some interest by ATF if you're continually buying assault weapons, four or five at a time, even if it is done legally. Then they just kill the business owner, make it look like an armed robbery, move on somewhere else and start all over again."

"You know, Muntze, this all sounds reasonable, but again, why don't you, and I, let the cops handle it?"

"When I told the locals in Tulsa what I knew, they locked up the liquor store guy immediately. I tried to offer him my services to get him out, but the courts ordered him held without bail. Keep in mind this guy, a really nice guy named Johnson, never had any kind of legal trouble before this in his life. While they had him in lockup, they let El Elegido slip out of town and out of the state. They put him in general population of a county lockup and, after a couple of weeks, Johnson turns up dead, stabbed through the heart. The official report called it the result of a fight with an unidentified inmate. I don't think this guy had ever been in a fight in his whole life."

"So you think the authorities were somehow involved in this guy getting stabbed in jail?" I ask.

"I couldn't say that," Muntze answers. "But what I can say for sure is that once I let the local authorities in on what El Elegido was doing, and what my interest in the mess was, they seemed all to happy to dump the whole thing on some little liquor store owner just struggling to keep his business going. Then he ends up dead, while in custody. Maybe he was just easier to tap for the thing than an outlaw motorcycle club with machine guns. I don't know. But I'm telling you these guys are well connected, both in Mexico and the US."

My head is spinning. What a perfect storm I've stepped into. As we both remain quiet for a long moment while I try to digest what Muntze is telling me, an older-model, rough-looking pickup truck pulls up outside. Muntze and I are standing alone at the front of the showroom, which is all walled in glass. I can see from there easily that it is the El Elegido that I only know as Texas at the wheel. "What's it going to be, Mike?" Muntze asks with his gaze on Texas and the truck.

Interstate Motorcycles

"I'm going to need to think."

"Have you mailed out any checks yet?"

"No, not yet!" I snap at him.

"Where is the money?"

"I deposited some of it, only what I needed, and I spent it. The bulk of it I still have in cash, just the way they brought it in."

"You don't have much time to think. They are going to be looking at picking up their guns today or tomorrow and if the money isn't there, it's going to be bad for you."

Texas crawls out of the pickup and starts walking toward the front door near where we are standing. "Here," Muntze tells me, thrusting a business card at me. "It's my cell phone number. Call soon. Tell me what you decide to do." Then he slides the aviators back on, zips up the jacket, and leaves the store. He and Texas manage to look like they are ignoring each other as they pass at the doorway.

On the passenger side of the old truck is a new face, a dark-skinned black man who stares straight ahead, waiting. Bob Culp was usually with Texas when he comes in. "Where's Bob?" I ask Texas, playing ignorant. The police investigating his gruesome murder have not yet released Culp's name publicly.

"None of your business!" he shouts while entering the building. "Did you send that money like we told you?" Lying, I say, "Yes, I did."

"All of it?"

"Of course, all of it."

"Good." Tossing another envelope on the sales desk, he says, "Get this deposited as soon as possible. Any questions?"

"Yeah, where's my cut?"

"You take that up with Escajada."

"Who?" I ask.

"Escajada is the Mexican that told you where to send the money. You got a problem with your cut, take it up with him."

"This isn't the deal I signed up for. I thought you guys were renting shop space from me to sell motorcycle parts. What gives?"

"We changed the damn deal!" Texas shouts.

"What if I don't want it changed?" I shout back.

As the conversation heats up between Texas and me, a marked police car pulls in. It's Detective Peterson, this time by himself. Texas sees the car and hastily leaves. "Get that deposited," he growls as he heads for the door.

"Sure, sure, right away, I've got it," I mumble once Texas is out of range of hearing. The arrival of Peterson now completes the circle. All of the lunatics in my life have been in to see me already this morning.

"Where's your partner?" I ask as the detective comes in.

"My partner? Do you mean detective Robb? He's not actually my regular partner. He works for the DEA and I work

Interstate Motorcycles

for the county. We were working on the Culp murder case together yesterday. He has been working a federal investigation of Culp for a couple of months now."

"For what?"

"I probably shouldn't say, but he is dead now so I guess it doesn't matter. They liked him for selling dope, mostly marijuana and cocaine. They were just about to link him to his source for the stuff, and we find him brutally murdered. That's why I wanted to stop by and talk to you some more, Mike. You see, we know that he was involved with some bad guys, but somehow you seem to be in the middle of that involvement."

"I'm in the middle?"

"Yeah, from what we can tell, he first met the guys we suspect he was getting the dope from while he worked here for you."

"You have that backward, Detective Peterson."

"What do you mean?"

"He introduced the club to us when he began to prospect for them just a few weeks ago."

"Club?" the detective asks.

"Right. El Elegido. The club."

"So they are the source of the dope?"

"Oh, I don't know. You said he met them here, didn't you?"

115

"No, I didn't say anything about a club. I just said it looks to us that he met his dope connections, whoever they are, about the time he worked here for you. So you think this *club*, El Elegido, is his source?"

"Detective, I completely do not know where or how Bob Culp was getting drugs. To be honest with you, I never would have given him credit for having enough ambition to sell drugs."

"I see." The detective pauses, biting his lower lip and checking his notes. "Um, you haven't made any unusual bank deposits recently, have you, Mike?"

That's a random leap from one subject to another. "What do you mean, *unusual?*"

"Yeah, you know, like unusually large, all cash deposits?"

"I'm a merchant, Detective Peterson. Ideally, I make deposits every day."

"But nothing out of the ordinary lately?"

"All of our deposits have been a little unusual this month."

"What do you mean?"

"We have just changed banks."

"Why would you do that? Someone offer you a better deal?"

"No. The bank we've been with unilaterally decided to sever our relationship. We are still setting up our accounts with the new bank. That together with a couple of late-season

Interstate Motorcycles

motorcycle sales for cash has created some deposits that might appear *unusual.*"

"Well, that makes sense, and you of course have the documentation on these bike sales."

"Would you like for me to get that together for you?"

"Well, not right now, but I will need that stuff for my report. If I come back in a few days, do you think it would be possible for you to provide me with copies of those sales?"

"I'm sure we can do that," I answer.

"Great! I really appreciate your cooperation on this matter, Mr. Douglas. I'm sure we will be able to wrap this thing up in a week or two. Thank you."

"You bet." As quickly as he arrived, he exits. As I watch Peterson drive off, I notice Muntze's Acura is still on the lot. He stayed till Texas and Peterson were both gone and then slowly pulls away.

I thumb through El Elegido's cash once I am alone in the store: another forty-two hundred dollars, as usual in mixed denominations. I put it in the file cabinet where I've kept the rest of the cash that I have not used. Up till today, the club has brought in a total of twenty-one thousand dollars including the money Chainsaw had brought in originally. I have deposited, and spent on my own expenses, three thousand dollars, leaving enough to send out the eighteen thousand dollars that the Mexican, Escajada, wants me to mail. That eighteen thousand along with today's new cash leaves me holding exactly twenty-two thousand, two hundred dollars for El Elegido. Something is going to have to break this logjam loose and, for better or worse, it's up to me to make the move.

It's the classic golden rule: the one holding the gold makes the rules. Unfortunately, none of the options in front of me look very appealing. If I send checks to the gun stores, they get their dope money cleaned up and get their weapons purchased and I either end up in prison or dead. If I turn myself over to Peterson and come clean about the whole twisted plot, I still end up in prison but perhaps for a shorter time, and then I end up dead when El Elegido puts out a prison contract on me. Then there is Greg Muntze. Tim Walker is the only guy I really know, and trust, out of all the players here. He has been a good friend and I've always known him to be a straight shooter. He wouldn't put me together with him if he believed Muntze was just full of crap. So if I pay Muntze the twenty-two thousand and he *gets rid* of my problem, I don't end up in prison, and I don't end up dead—if he can actually pull it off. That's a big *if*. What if Muntze is just smooth enough to con Walker and me, take the twenty-two thousand, go back to New Mexico, and live happily ever after? Or, what if El Elegido actually kills him while he is trying to get rid of them? Either way, I do not land in prison, but my corpse will probably never be found. Still, Muntze looks like the most appealing solution. I call him at the number he left with me and he returns within minutes.

"Hello again, Mike," he says as he enters, looking from side to side. "I see you had another El Elegido visit. What did they want?"

"Same as always: dropping off cash."

"You didn't turn the cash over to the detectives either."

"How do you know that?"

"You're not in jail. You knew the guy they killed yesterday, Culp, right?"

Interstate Motorcycles

"Yeah, I knew him."

"He was dead as soon as he got hooked up with them. They only used him as leverage to find and then attach themselves to a guy like you. Once you were hooked, his fate was sealed and the more gruesome his death, the better. It makes it easier to control you and the others they've got their teeth into."

"You mean there are others? Around here?"

"Oh, yeah."

"Who?"

"I don't know for certain, but I am certain that they are still looking to expand."

"All you want is the cash, right?"

"Yes, I want these dirtbags' cash."

I reach into the drawer and toss an envelope full of bills on the desk in front of Muntze. "How much is in there?" he asks.

"Eleven thousand dollars."

"How much are you holding, Mike?"

"A little more than that."

"I am going to have to have it all."

"You get the rest when I see some results. Look, I don't know you or anything about you. You flash me some kind of a badge, tell me some wild story about drug cartels and outlaw bike clubs, people getting wacked in jail, and law enforcement seemingly involved in it. We have mutilated bodies showing up and detectives looking at me for it. Hell, Muntze, my brain is swimming here. What would make me believe that you aren't shaking me down for all of it so you can split and leave me hanging in the wind? I'll be the one with no head tomorrow."

Muntze smiles. "All right, we'll call this a down payment. You see me work, I get the rest. Got it?"

"Fair enough. You say you can make this go away. Well, then, make it go away!"

"I'll be in touch, Mike. I just want to warn you it is going to get violent. There's no other way. But I am going to take care of it. Trust me. Try not to worry. If anyone from the club gets in touch with you, just play it carefully. Keep them thinking you're okay with this whole arrangement and that you are doing everything they ask you to do. You're doing the right thing. I know this all seems crazy to you right now, but you have made the only good choice you have left, which is to handle it *my way*." Muntze disappears. I pray I'm doing the right thing.

A month ago I was just a small motorcycle dealer in a college town in rural Missouri, struggling to keep things afloat, and the biggest legal problem I had was a speeding ticket. How can things get this fouled up, this fast? It's finally setting in on me. I've got my wife hidden out of town and Bob Culp, who, although a loser was harmless, is now dead, viciously killed by the guys he left me doing business with. I should have known better, but I needed the cash. Everything I have, everything I've ever worked for, is represented by this crazy little motorcycle shop. Not much, I know, but it's a living, it's mine, and it's all I've got. Feels like its all slipping away from me faster now than ever.

Interstate Motorcycles

The emotion of the thing starts to engulf me, a blend of anger, tension from too many hours, not enough money, and no sleep. I miss Lori. She hasn't even been gone a full day yet and the loneliness chokes me. She is away, Adam is at home recovering, the customers who are the lifeblood of our store are away because of both the time of year and an economy that is crushing everyone. It's just me now and my strength wanes. I feel emptied out at a time when I need to be vigorous. Tired at a time when I must be clear headed so I don't make any more mistakes. The stakes are high and getting higher. No longer is it simply a matter of *Will my business and my way of life survive?* But now it is questionable whether or not I will even survive.

For the first time in my life, I think I can truly empathize with what Dad went through when the dairy closed and robbed him of his livelihood. After the morning that the union let him down with finding a new job, he stopped leaving the house. He just could not believe that they couldn't help him out. I don't think he showered, shaved, or changed out of his pajamas for a solid month. Dad always liked to have a few drinks, but nothing like this. I don't think I ever saw him sober again. He had been a dairy delivery manager for twenty years, through the end of the era when people got their milk delivered. In his world, he believed if he kept his nose to the grindstone and did his best on the job every day, he would have that job till he retired. That's just what he believed. It never occurred to him that something like this could ever happen. When it did, it was devastating. It shook his faith in how life worked, and he eventually stopped believing in everything.

He had always insisted that the whole family was in church together every Sunday morning and every Wednesday night. Our family would always take our place in the center section, near the front like we owned it. He was straight and proud during the dairy years in that place, surrounded by his family in our church worshiping the God that he was sure loved him.

He was confident that God's blessings poured down on him because of his obedience and faithfulness. He taught me that not only in words but by how he lived his life. He served in leadership on the church council and on the board of elders. He was well liked and respected by the congregation, and he gave generously. So generously sometimes that he and my mom argued over it. When she would rebuke him for big offerings, he would explain to her that it was God's anyway and she shouldn't worry about it. At the end, he would smile and hug her and tell her not to worry. "God will provide, God will always provide."

After that first unemployed month, he cleaned himself up one morning, put on his church clothes, and went in search of a new job, but there simply was none. A young man couldn't find work at the time, let alone a fifty-year-old guy who only had one skill, and it wasn't marketable anymore. His friends at church kept telling him it would be all right. They told him to pray harder and that they knew how he felt. They patted his back, told him to keep the faith and pray, but they never offered him a job, and several of them could have. They didn't know, or care, how he felt. They slowly drifted away, watching him fade. He associated their abandonment to his inability to give generously anymore, and so do I. He continued attending worship through it all, but started drinking even more.

Six months after the dairy closed, out of unemployment benefits and still unable to find a more suitable position, he went to work at the corner gas station for his friend Mr. Petrowski. Hugh Petrowski wasn't a churchgoer. He cussed a lot and was as coarse and rough as a bastard file, but he was the only one to throw Dad a lifeline when he was drowning. He worked alongside Moony pumping gas, cleaning the glass, and checking under hoods. He did his best to keep his head up and a smile on his face, especially around me, but it broke him slowly, little by little every day. Not because the job was bad—he was

Interstate Motorcycles

proud to be working again—or because Mr. Petrowski wasn't fair to him. It was because the life he had so much faith in had simply dissolved, and he missed it unbearably.

But he never threw in with drug dealers either. As the life I have fought so hard to build dissolves, I think he would be ashamed of me for the choices I've made this month. As much as I wanted to run off and hide from all of this, I was suffering from the fruits of my own bad decisions and I was just going to have to handle it. I am banking that this bail bondsman is on the up and up, but I've given up on trusting anyone.

I take a deep breath and put an end to the pity party right there. Muntze's parting words ring in my mind: "It's going to be violent." It already has been. Through the years I have accumulated three pistols that I keep in drawers and under counters scattered around the store. One is a Smith & Wesson snub-nosed .357 magnum revolver that I have a permit to carry, loaded with heavy, hollow-point rounds. Accurate out to about thirty or forty feet, each of the six shells in the cylinder is more than adequate to eliminate whatever target they find. Another is a nickel-plated .25 semi-auto ultra-light with a nine-round magazine. Not too intimidating, but it has a high rate of fire enabling it to be emptied with every round clustered into the size of a paper plate in less than ten seconds. The last is a .32 over and under pocket derringer that could be hidden in the palm of your hand, loaded with an illegal round that used to be marketed as a Dragon Fire. The lightweight bullet is made of hollow lead, filled with bird shot, and capped with a hard wax tip. The idea is for the bullet to puncture its target making a small hole, then for the tip to explode on impact. Only accurate from four or five feet away, this thing is intended for hand-to-hand combat. I hope I don't need it. I checked, cleaned, and reloaded the weapons, evaluating their placement around the store. If one of my many adversaries comes to kill me, I am at least determined to make it a fight.

December 18, 2009

Friday morning, one week before Christmas Day, and the weather is still cooperating. The sky is clear, the sun is bright, but it's still too cold for riding motorcycles. I hope the sunny skies bring out the shoppers on this last weekend before Christmas. I spent the night before lonely without Lori, and mostly sleepless, thinking too much. I should have been thinking about discounts and last-minute holiday specials I could run. Perhaps I should have been consumed with the real meaning of gift giving during the Christmas season anyway. But instead, I was consumed with thoughts of El Elegido and the county sheriff's office detective I'm playing cat and mouse with. None of that matters now. I'm in the shop and we're open for business and I have to make the best of it.

I carefully place the pistols, which I cleaned and checked yesterday, in locations I think will be most strategic. The .357 is now in the right-hand drawer of the sales desk in the center of the showroom where I am usually seated. From that location, this weapon can cover the entire retail area with deadly accuracy. The .25 auto is under the keyboard of the computer

Interstate Motorcycles

on the parts counter where all parts and accessory sales are completed. That is the second most likely place for me to be throughout the day and would be the logical place for the small pistol to be most effective. The derringer is loaded and in the pocket of my trousers. I sure hope it stays there.

Everything I can make ready is ready for whatever the day brings. Sitting at the sales desk alone, looking upward at nothing in particular, I say, "Lord, I know I've been out of touch with you lately, and I'm not so sure that you will hear from me now. I couldn't really blame you for holding a grudge. I'm sorry though, and I'm asking for forgiveness for all of my faults and, my sins. I want you to know that I never intended to separate myself from you but only to get some space from church people. You know the type I mean, Lord: exploiters and self-righteous busybodies watching everyone else's every move. I have just tried to do the right thing, make an honest living, take care of the people who are counting on me, and try to love you like my dad did. That does not seem like it should be too much to want. Whether I live to see tomorrow or not, Lord, I'm praying you will hold me by the hand. The Bible says whatever we ask, ask in Jesus's name and it will be heard. I'm holding you to that promise now, in Jesus's name I pray."

The front door chimes—last-minute Christmas gift shoppers. I'm glad to see them. In fact the whole morning is mildly busy, keeping my mind off the money laundering drama and back where it belongs: just being a good motorcycle dealer. It was enjoyable but short lived. Early afternoon a familiar old Chevy Impala arrives. Bob's old car, with two equally familiar faces: Texas and Escajada the Mexican. They both enter the currently empty showroom. Neither of them is wearing his colors this time. Both are dressed in farm clothes like they are headed out to feed cattle. Their faces do not look like they intend for this to be a friendly visit.

"Mr. Mike," Escajada begins the conversation. "I think we have a problem here."

The two slowly circle the outside edge of the store's floor in opposite directions, both keeping their eyes locked on me. "What would that be?" I ask.

"You didn't send out that money, Mr. Mike, did you?"

"What makes you say that?"

"Are you trying to be funny?" Texas joins in. I move slowly away from the Mexican who is standing about fifteen feet from me and closer to the sales desk where the Smith & Wesson is stashed.

"What do you mean I didn't mail the checks?"

Looking at the floor and stroking his thin mustache with his thumb and forefinger, slightly shaking his head, he says, "Are you trying to treat me like an idiot? If you had done what we expected, the checks would have arrived yesterday. I gave you the courtesy of an extra day, and now I find out from my associates that they were not delivered again today. Mr. Mike, it never takes longer than two days for the checks to arrive. Do you want to explain to me why there are still no checks today? And, if you shuffle any closer to that desk, I am going to shoot your foot right where you are," he says, slowly sliding what looks like a fully automatic pistol with an extended assault magazine protruding from the bottom of the grip. He slowly lowers the weapon down to his hip and points it toward me. "Yes, Mr. Mike, in the foot, which will be extraordinarily painful and will keep you right where you are."

"I'm not moving" are the only words I can squeeze through my constricted vocal cords, trying desperately to stay calm and

Interstate Motorcycles

wondering where my eleven-thousand-dollar bodyguard has gone.

"Just shoot him, Emilio," Texas says as he laughs while facing me from his position just inside the front door. I notice he is also holding a pistol. They have me in a cross fire.

"We are going to shoot you many times today, Mr. Mike, in painful ways that will kill you slowly. I will make sure the pain lasts as long as it takes for you to give me back every dollar of my money."

Escajada and I are watching each other intently and he keeps the pistol pointed at my legs. Backing slowly toward the open business office door, he says, "Where is you're pretty woman, Mike? She must suffer too for your foolishness. Do you think we will not find her?" He glances momentarily away from me and into her darkened, empty office. Surveying her empty chair, his head begins to snap back toward me when the uneasy quietness of the deadly encounter is suddenly shattered by the sharp, explosive sound of rapid gun fire and shattering glass coming from the area of the front door.

I dive to the floor and take cover behind the nearest motorcycle while pulling the derringer from my pocket. The submachine gun in the Mexican's hand instantly goes to work with deafening efficiency, blowing the rest of the glass of the front door and wall out onto the parking lot. A millisecond later the spray of deadly bullets is destroying the wall, windows, and all of our motorcycles and inventory in the showroom, sweeping toward me. I thrust the small derringer under the crankcase of the Moto Guzzi I'm lying behind and empty it toward the Mexican's ankles. Suddenly I hear rapid snaps of pistol fire again coming from the area where the front door was. Then an eerie silence.

"Are you hit? Douglas! Are you hit?" It's Greg Muntze crouched near the front door with a Glock nine millimeter raised to shoulder level, clenched in gloved hands and sweeping deliberately from right to left across the store's field of fire.

I pop up first facing Escajada, who lies face up in a growing pool of his own blood. Then I turn toward Muntze who is now on one knee alongside the facedown Texas who is missing most of his head. "He's not going anywhere. Are you okay?" Muntze says, deliberately moving toward Escajada's body with the Glock still trained on him.

"Yes, yes, I am." I have to force the words through my constricted throat as if unseen hands are squeezing. I have to remind myself to breathe. Breathe! As I pull the air in, the strong sulfur smell of cordite burns my sinuses. Good Lord, what has happened? Muntze inspects the motionless Mexican carefully before lowering the piece toward the floor. Two small holes in the upper center of the Carhartt work jacket, one on either side of the zipper. One small black hole is square in the center of the Mexican's exposed throat. The body lies in a large, almost brown blood bath pouring from the exit wounds. One black eye on the lifeless face is half open and the other is closed. Muntze places the hot Glock on the floor next to his victim's corpse. "Call nine-one-one and report multiple shots fired at this location. Request uniforms and an ambulance. They will be here fast."

I step carefully over the grotesque grease spot on the floor and carefully into the business office, then dial emergency services as if being guided by someone, or something else.

"Did you get a couple shots off from the floor?" he asks. "I told you to let me handle it. Looks like you actually made contact." He points at the bloody groove notched on the side of his left ankle.

Interstate Motorcycles

"Well, where the hell were you?" I shout back, pointing down at the wound. "That wouldn't have kept him from killing me."

"You've been safe since you gave me the deposit. Just because you didn't see doesn't mean I haven't been near you. I had you staked out from beside the building all day." There is a stack of plywood crating material, wooden pallets, and old tires we've removed from customers' bikes, which he stacked neatly to take cover in, leaving him a clear perspective of the entire front parking lot where everyone enters and exits. "I got here and set up a hide in the wee hours this morning. Once our boys here were in the building, I slid around to the front. Seeing through the window that their weapons were out and that this clown had his back to me, I went to work. I put two in the back of this one's head and then emptied my first magazine toward the Mexican before hitting the floor behind that stack of new tires to reload. When he directed his fire in your direction, I had an easy shot."

I scan the wreckage of our neat and well-ordered showroom. Every window on the front wall and door is blown out into a pile of shattered glass on the asphalt. All of the windows on the south wall, where my desk is located, are also missing and the surrounding walls are heavily damaged. Merchandise that we have always taken great pain to keep organized for our customers is now shredded and strewn around the floor. New helmets are now shattered on their shelves, and on many of our new motorcycles I can see holes and missing and damaged parts. It's like a metal typhoon has blown through.

"What a mess," I say in disbelief.

"Douglas, look at me. The police will be here in a minute. They will take us both in and question us separately about what happened. We need to tell the same story, got it?

Bill Dunkus

"They already know I've been working the area for a bail jumper in El Elegido wanted in New Mexico. I filed notice with the county as soon as I got to Missouri. They also know that El Elegido has been working on you, but they do not know you've taken any money. You will tell them that they solicited you with the cash but you wouldn't go along!

"Our explanation on the shooting will be that I was tailing these two and followed them here. They know I've been snooping around you already. I see my boys through the window with weapons drawn, threatening you because you have not been willing to get involved, so I go to work. The rest speaks for itself. You got it now!"

"Yeah, I have it."

"Say it back to me," he says as the sirens converge from all directions onto the parking lot.

"They wanted me to take cash, I wouldn't do it, you've been snooping around for a bail jumper, they show today threatening me for not going along with them, and you show up in the nick of time and kill both of them."

"Don't screw it up," Muntze says as police run in through the wreckage of the front door, guns drawn, shouting for Muntze and me to show our hands. We both comply. "Is anyone else in the building?" A uniformed officer with weapon drawn yells.

I answer, "No."

Detective Peterson is one of the first to arrive. He approaches us with his revolver in his hand. "Is this your work, Greg?" he asks Muntze as if they were old friends.

Interstate Motorcycles

"They were going to kill him," he answers, nodding toward me. "I'm unarmed. That's my nine millimeter on the floor next to the Mexican. I have the carry permit and registration in my wallet."

"Are you two all right?" a uniformed officer asks, leaning over to examine Escajada.

"Yes," we both respond in unison.

Within minutes the wreckage of my motorcycle shop is filled with police officers and emergency medical services personnel. They're searching everywhere, carefully clearing the whole building. Muntze was right: they separated us immediately. "Mike, why don't you come over here to the office and sit down. You look a little shaky," Peterson suggests, resting a hand on my shoulder.

"I'm all right," I answer, but I sit down at Lori's desk in the business office anyway. Peterson holsters his revolver and stays right beside me.

"We are taking this one in to get a statement," an officer tells Peterson while his partner escorts Muntze to their patrol car.

"Mike," Peterson says, taking a knee alongside my chair, "we are going to need you to come in with us too. Is there anyone who can stay around here to get the place secured?"

"Let me give Adam Bower a call. I think he will do it."

Adam agrees to get here as soon as he can, and Detective Peterson assigns a couple of deputies to stay around until the place is safe. One of the deputies gives me a phone number for a local board-up service, where an employee says he can have someone here in an hour.

"Are you ready, Mike?"

"Yeah, I guess so."

As Peterson and I leave, the whole place is still buzzing with investigators snapping photos, numbering spent shell cases on the floor, and sectioning off areas around where the dead El Elegido were. They've been removed but their fluids remain. Police outside are blocking off the parking lot, preventing nosy passersby from coming in to snoop around. "We'll keep everyone back," Peterson reassures me as we pull away.

While driving toward the police station, the shock of the shooting sets in on me. But I'm still alive. "Thank you, Lord," I whisper in the backseat of the cruiser. It's a short drive but it seems long.

All of the personnel at the station make an effort to relax me by their tone and manners. My first stop is at a desk where I'm fingerprinted. The deputy processing my prints tells me they need them just to separate mine from others they're taking in the investigation. Then I'm seated in a comfortable chair in an austere little office. "I've never been interrogated before," I say to Peterson, who has hovered close to me since he got to the shop.

"You're not being interrogated now either, Mike. We just need to find out what happened in your store today. You are not under arrest and you're free to leave any time you want. Okay? Would you like a bottle of water or a cup of coffee or something?"

"No, thanks."

Interstate Motorcycles

"Would you mind if I record our conversation, just so I can use the recording for my report when I put it together?"

"I don't mind," I answer.

"So, what can you tell me?"

"This outfit, El Elegido, asked me to handle some cash for them."

"Handle?"

"Yes, they wanted me to deposit their cash into my business account."

"Why?"

"All they would tell me was that they needed for me to send checks, from my account, out to people at their direction."

"Did you take any cash?"

"No."

"Why did they think you would deposit random cash into your account?"

"They offered me a percentage of the cash as payment for the service."

"Interesting," Peterson says, scribbling a note on a yellow legal pad. "Pretty easy money, huh, Mike?"

"It sounded more like sleazy money to me, Detective."

"So what happened today that caused a lethal gunfight at your motorcycle shop?"

"They stopped in and tried to intimidate me into cooperating with them. I told them I would not. They drew their weapons."

"Where was Muntze when that happened?"

"I don't know. All I know for sure is about the time I really believed they might shoot me, he burst through the glass door shooting at them."

"Don't you think it's a little odd that he just happened to be there at that moment?"

"Not really."

"Why not?" Peterson asks with a shocked tone in his voice.

"He has been snooping around my shop ever since this El Elegido bunch first showed up about a month ago. He told me he was tracking one of them who had jumped bail and wanted me to know that I might see him hanging around sometimes."

"Have you seen him *hanging around?*"

"Yeah, the guy gave me the creeps, but I'm sure glad he was there today."

"I'll bet you are. He's former special forces and apparently a pretty good shot."

"Do you know him?" I ask.

Interstate Motorcycles

"No, not really, he checked in with us on his bail jumper when he got to town, and I've met up with him a few times since then at various places. We both seemed to be following the same guys around. He looks like he's legitimate to me.

"Mike, I'm just wondering why you didn't tell me that these guys were threatening you when I first talked to you about El Elegido?"

"At that time, I didn't think there was a threat. They were just a pain in my butt, like I told you then, and I wanted to be rid of them. They were bad for business."

"Well," Peterson says studying the legal pad and tapping his ink pen on the desk, "I think that's about all I need from you. Why don't you just relax here for a few minutes and I will get you a ride back to your shop."

After sitting in the little room alone for a while, I start feeling like the suspect in a television cop show who's being watched by the cops in another room on a hidden camera. Remembering that I am not being held, I leave the room and walk the long hallway back to the station's lobby.

"Mike," Peterson says as I approach the desk, "I was just coming back to get you. I'll take you back to your shop if you're up to going back. Do you want me to run you by the hospital to get checked out first?"

"No, I've got to get back there and start picking up the pieces."

"I hear you. Let's go."

It's a quiet drive back, just Peterson and me, and I'm in the front seat. I feel a lot less like a suspect. "It's quite a mess," Peterson says as we pull onto the parking lot.

He's right. The board-up company is just finishing up its work, leaving the whole front and south side of the building covered in plywood. The millions of specks of shattered tempered glass are still scattered everywhere. Around the plywood, a yellow ribbon is draped with "Police Line" printed repeatedly in ten-inch intervals. The front door had sustained enough damage so that it is inoperable and had to be completely boarded over, so I have to enter from around the back, through the service department. Adam is back there when I come in. He just looks at me with very sad eyes.

"We're going to be okay," I tell him. "We will put the place back together again."

"The showroom is still a huge mess. I wanted to clean up a little but the cops said not to touch anything."

"That's best for now. Are you all right?"

"Yeah, it's just, you know, crazy. Really crazy! The floor up front is covered in blood. Are you okay? The cops said you weren't hurt."

"I'm fine."

"The board-up guys said to give you this bill," Adam says as he hands me an envelope. "They said your insurance company should pay it."

"Thanks. I appreciate you coming over for me and keeping things together. I can handle it from here if you want to take off. Do I owe you anything for coming in?"

Interstate Motorcycles

"No. Do you need me to come in tomorrow and help you get the place cleaned up?"

"No. I think we will be closed for a week or two."

"All right, well, let me know if I can help out."

Adam was right; the showroom is a huge mess. The police had cleared the building and left, leaving only one deputy still parked out front. I am the last one here. I walk slowly around, making mental notes on all that needs to be done, making my way back to the file cabinet where I hid the cash. It is still there in the bank envelope, right where I left it. It's dusk, about the time we would normally close anyhow, and I'm really tired, ready to go home and have a cocktail. I turn out the lights, set the alarm, and lock up on my way out the back, giving the deputy a wave as I get into my old pickup truck to head home.

December 19, 2009
The Day After

I CAN'T STAY AWAY FROM the place, even though I know nothing will be going on. I call Lori from the shop to tell her what happened.

"I didn't call you last night because it was late, I was tired, it was all over, and it would only have kept you up all night with worry."

"I'll check into a flight back today," she answers.

"No, don't do that. I'm more anxious than ever to get out of town now."

"I'll be worried sick until you get here, until I get my arms around you."

"I know, I miss you too, but there's nothing to worry about now. The bad guys are dead. I'm safe and we will be all right."

"The store is a mess, huh?"

"Yes, it is. I'm going to let you go for now and start straightening things up."

"I should be there to help!"

"Stay there. I'll get down right after Christmas as planned."

"All right, I will wait for you here if you promise me something."

"Sure."

"Go to church tomorrow, will you?"

"Sure, babe, I'll go to church. I promise. Love you."

My next call is to our insurance company who assures me that they will have an adjuster out today, even though it's Saturday. It's the least they can do, considering my premium.

I begin the rebuilding out front, shoveling up piles of broken glass, and, of course once people see me, they drive in and line up to ask what happened. The telling and retelling of the shooting turns an hour-long job into three hours, but a few do help out with the shoveling, which I appreciate.

Once the front is tidied up, I excuse myself and go inside to get things organized. I don't want friends and customers inside, confronted with the bloody floor. I ask them to bear with me and stay outside. The morbid curiosity of a few gets the best of them and they strain to see through any seams in the board-up windows. Inside I begin the slow process of picking up and moving motorcycles around to clean, being careful not to disturb the police tape marking off where the bodies were. There is so much crime tape in the room the work goes slowly. Hearing the rear service department door slam shut, I shout, "Please stay outside for me! It's a mess up here."

"I've already seen it," Muntze replies, stepping from behind the parts counter. "How are you making it, Mike?"

"Good, I think, although it's going to take some time to get my store back together."

"You'll be bigger and better than ever by next spring."

"How about you, how are you making it?" I ask him.

"Me? I'm fine. The sheriff's department is still checking my credentials with New Mexico and hasn't released me to leave yet. I should be cleared by the end of the day, and then I'm headed home."

"No more El Elegido to track down?"

"Escajada and Southerland were the main players up here. The rest of the bunch they had around them were dopers, hookers, prospects, and wannabes. With the leaders dead, the rest of that crowd has vaporized."

"Southerland?"

"The guy you called Texas was a guy named Rueben Southerland, a real piece of work. He had outstanding warrants all over the southwest for everything from human trafficking to capital murder. You need to start picking your friends more carefully."

Interstate Motorcycles

"He was no friend of mine," I answer. "So the rest of them are gone? I've been wondering who I should start watching for next."

"They are all gone."

"For now," I say skeptically. "What about this big drug cartel you told me about?"

"You aren't going to have to worry about them either. Escajada and Southerland were getting careless and stupid. They were skimming the dope for their own use and blowing cash as if it was theirs. The Mexicans were about to rid themselves of those two anyway. They are not going to waste time and resources on a lousy twenty grand that those two corpses probably blew. Believe me! They have bigger fish to fry."

"I guess I owe you some money."

Looking down at the floor, Muntze grunts, "Yes, you do."

I remove the deposit envelope from the file cabinet with the balance of El Elegido's cash and hand it to him. "I appreciate the help."

"Glad I was here to do it for you. Stay out of trouble, will you?" Muntze speaks while thumbing through the bills.

"Listen, how about I fix you up with a new motorcycle while you're here? You can afford it"

"Oh, no, thanks, Mike. This money is earmarked for something else a little more serious."

"Really, new car?"

Bill Dunkus

"No, nothing like that," he answers me, still thumbing through the cash. "I'm going to give it to Johnson's widow."

"Johnson?"

"The liquor store owner near Tulsa that got shanked while in jail on a drug sales charge."

"That's who the money is for?" I ask, surprised.

"Yeah, that's what I wanted the money for from the beginning. I liked Johnson, but I got to him too late. I still feel bad about it. Here," he looks up from thumbing through the cash and hands me five hundred dollars. "You can probably use some of this yourself."

I should refuse the money, but don't. I fold the bills and stuff them in my pocket.

"I have to get going," he says.

"Take care," I tell him, shaking his hand. "I'll see you around sometime, right?"

"I don't think so," he answers with a smile. "Not unless you need a good bail bondsman."

I've only known the guy a few days, but as the back door slams behind him I feel like I've just said good-bye to an old friend.

December 20, 2009

Sunday morning and I'm going to church. For one thing, I promised Lori that I would, to keep her in Pensacola. But mainly because I'm not dead and probably should be. I have an overwhelming desire to show up in a house of God and tell him, "Thanks."

I'm hoping that folks here will give me a little space about the shooting at my store. I would really like to just spend the worship time checked in with God, not every other nosy body in the building. I guess it's too much to ask for.

I walk through the front door and am instantly descended upon with the same questions as I've been getting since the shots were fired: "What happened?" "How are you?" "Do you need anything?" But by now I can tell my story in one rote sentence.

"They tried to kill me, but a bail bondsman who was stalking them killed them first, and they made a big mess out of my store."

I wish I had made a sign to bring with me that I could just walk through the hallways with so I could stop saying it. After the service, the young pastor seeks me out. A nice enough, plump Irish kid about half my age named Patrick Gallagher. Good preacher too. We don't know each other very well because of my lack of activity and sporadic, at best, Sunday attendance. But he knows Lori quite well because of her commitment here.

"Mike, you doing all right?" he asks as I'm moving through the crowd for the door.

"Yeah, Reverend, I'll make it."

"Please, just call me Patrick. Do you have a minute?"

"I don't know, Patrick. I'm kind of in a hurry." It isn't true. I'm going home to get drunk again this afternoon. I just do not want to be grilled anymore about what happened.

"I'll be brief. Come into my office for a minute."

This guy has a well-deserved reputation for persistence. I'm not going to be able to get away so I might as well get it over with. "Sure, what's up?"

We swoop around the corner and into his office and he closes the door behind us. "Have a seat, Mike. I just want to get to know you a little better. I guess you've become quite a celebrity?"

"Nothing to it. Just have a gunfight go down in your motorcycle shop, huh?" I'm trying to be funny but he doesn't really laugh, just returned an odd look to me and a *Mona Lisa* smile. "I'm just kidding."

Interstate Motorcycles

"How's Lori?"

Well, that makes sense. He is really interested in how she is doing. "Oh, of course. I should have told you straight away. She's all right. She's been in Florida visiting her sister and she was not at work when the shooting took place. She would be here this morning as usual if she was in town."

"I knew that. She told me she was going to be gone on vacation before she left. She called me at home last night, said you would be here this morning, and asked if I would make sure that you were okay. She seemed seriously worried."

"I love that woman. She is looking after me from a thousand miles away. Really, Patrick, I'm going to be fine. I just want to try to get this thing behind me. You know?"

"Yeah, yeah, sure, sure, I completely understand that. I'm sure you will be fine too. It will just take a bit of time. She wanted me to make sure of that, obviously. But Mike, she is concerned about you at an even deeper level. I think she is worried that something inside of you has been hurting for a long time, much longer than since the shooting took place."

"You mean my lack of regular church attendance?"

"No, not really. I think that your lack of regular church attendance is just one of the symptoms of the deeper hurting that I'm talking about."

"It's refreshing to be having a conversation that is not centered on what happened at the shop Friday."

"I imagine you're getting sick of hearing and talking about it."

"You have no idea."

"So, how's everything else? Why do you think you haven't been a regular attendee for worship? Don't like my preaching?"

"No, that's not it. You're a nice guy, Patrick. Lori has nothing but good things to say about you. I don't have a beef with you, but some of the other people around here . . ."

"They are just people too. Same as me, same as you. Nobody is perfect, you know?"

"I'm not looking for perfection, just a little sincerity."

"What do you mean?"

"Well, I think this is the Lord's Day, isn't it?"

"Yes," Patrick responds, nodding.

"Most people seem to come to church more interested in turning the Lord's Day into being all about themselves rather than about the Lord. Seeming to be religious for what they can get out of it, rather than what they can give back."

"Some, perhaps. Why did you come this morning? Just because you promised Lori you would?"

"Yeah, that's part of it. I promised her I would, but I wanted to tell God, face to face on his day and in his house, that I'm grateful I survived the encounter at the shop."

"God wants to hear from us about everything, not just the major crises."

Interstate Motorcycles

"Pastor, you're a fine guy. I won't snow you. I can't promise you I'll be here every Sunday, but I can tell you this: I'll be here a lot more often than I have been."

"Good. I just want you to know before you leave that you have a friend here Mike. Me."

He stands and offers his hand. I like him even more. He treats my wife with respect and preaches a good message. "I appreciate that, Patrick," I say as I take his hand. "I'll be around."

"I'm looking forward to it."

As I drive up the long lane in front of my house, I'm caught by surprise to find a sheriff's deputy cruiser parked there. It's Tom Hughes, in uniform, at the wheel with Detective Peterson by his side. They exit the car as I pull in. "Hello, Mike," they say in sync. "How are you fellows doing today? What brings you to the house?"

"How's the cleanup at the shop going?" Tom asks. "I want to get my bike in to you for a full service before spring."

"The cleanup is going slow, but you can bring the bike in any time, Tom. Is that the only reason you guys came out?"

"No, Mike," Peterson jumps in. "I asked Tom to drive me over because I have some other questions for you about the shooting Friday. Would it be possible for us to go inside and talk a little? It won't take long."

Tom looks a little uncomfortable when Peterson asks the question, leaving me with the impression that Peterson really wants something more. I'm guessing he wants a look around

147

inside. "Sure, come on in," I answer, knowing there is nothing in the house to hide.

Lori and I live in a modest vinyl-sided, ranch-style house on a remote county highway. The two police officers follow me into the house through the garage, which is the entry we use most often. That doorway goes into a great room that combines the kitchen, dining room, and living room, all located beneath a vaulted ceiling with exposed rough-hewn oak beams. "Nice place you have here," Tom Hughes says as he makes a slow pass around the room, looking at the artwork on the walls. "Really nice," Peterson adds.

"You want to sit down?" I ask the detective, pulling a chair back at the dining room table.

"No thanks. We won't keep you long. There was something that came up while we were putting all of the pieces together in the report. I just wanted to ask you if you had a pistol at the shop on Friday."

"Well, actually I had three pistols at the shop Friday. They are always there and they are all registered properly."

"Yeah, we found the .357and the .25. What I mean to ask is, *Did you fire a pistol in the exchange on Friday?*"

"I fired the derringer from the floor."

"Well, we found the derringer on the floor. Of course it only had your prints on it. We were wondering why you didn't mention returning fire from your position when you gave us a statement at headquarters?"

"I don't know. I probably just overlooked it in the excitement."

Interstate Motorcycles

"Well, that makes sense all right," Peterson says in a comforting tone. "That makes perfect sense. Mike, are there any other details you may have overlooked?"

"No, I don't think so."

"Are you sure?" Peterson asks again, this time with a more serious tone. "I mean, shooting at someone is a pretty important detail. Could you have overlooked anything else?"

"Hey, Mike," Tom Hughes says from the fireplace behind me in the living room, "these are really nice." He is looking at two Civil War muzzle-loading rifles that I have hanging above the mantel. One is a Union infantry replica and the other a Confederate Poor Boy that I built myself from a kit. "May I take them down for a closer look?"

"Tom, I'd rather you didn't. They are just collectors and are up there for display."

"They aren't operational?" Tom asks, still examining the weapons.

"They are operational, but I don't hunt with them. They are for display only."

"Do you have any other rifles in the house?" Peterson asks.

"Yes."

"Pistols?"

"No, I only have pistols at the shop."

"Can we see the other rifles you own?" Peterson asks as Tom Hughes joins us.

"Yeah, I don't mind. They are in a gun safe in the back bedroom." Walking to the gun safe effectively gives them a tour of the whole house. They glance through every door as we walk together to the back. Inside of the safe are the .243 Remington 700 that I do hunt with, two shotguns, and a World War I-era Enfield .303.

"Here they are," I tell them, unlocking the safe and stepping out of the way.

"May I?" Peterson asks as he reaches into the safe.

"I don't mind," I answer.

The two police officers clear each weapon, making sure they are unloaded, and then look them over thoroughly. "No assault weapons though, huh, Mike?" Peterson asks, putting the weapons away in the safe.

"Not unless you consider the antique Enfield an assault weapon. This is all I own."

"The Enfield is a real beauty. It's not what I was referring to. I think that's it for now," Peterson says nodding to Tom Hughes. The two of them walk back up the hallway toward the living room, again looking into every open doorway.

"Thanks for the help, Mike," Tom Hughes says.

"Is there something particular you guys are looking for?" I ask abruptly. "Obviously you wanted to come in for a look around. What's up?"

Interstate Motorcycles

"Mike, we know this El Elegido bunch was involved in some weapons trafficking. You're not considered a suspect in any of that at this time, but we have to do a complete investigation. You look clean, just as we believed you would be, and we appreciate your cooperation. We will need to hang on to the derringer for a while for ballistics. If there is anything else you can tell us about the shooting Friday, anything else that you may have overlooked in the excitement, please let us know as soon as possible."

December 24, 2009

It seems like a long week has past since the shooting, and a busy one. Lots of work with insurance adjusters and contractors trying to get my motorcycle shop put back together again. It will take some time. Detective Peterson has been here several times, removing crime scene ribbon and asking the same question he left me with at the house on Sunday: "Have you forgotten anything else?" Adam had been in a couple of days helping out as much as possible with a broken arm. We got the floor cleaned, the damaged merchandise removed, and estimates prepared on the bullet damage to motorcycles. We even reworked the front door board-up so that it opens and closes. All of the glass has been ordered.

As far as business, this final workweek of the year has been slow: virtually no sales. A few customers have stopped in, but I really think they were more interested in just looking around rather than buying anything. It seems fitting to close the year out the same as it has been from the beginning: in the red. I was hoping for a bike to sell this week so I could pay a few bills but no such luck. At this point, I just want to get down to Pensacola

Interstate Motorcycles

and hug Lori. I miss her bad. A little time out of town, away from it all, sounds pretty good. Adam came in this morning, but I told him to go on home and spend Christmas Eve with his wife and kids. I think he's as worried about the business as Lori and I are. He likes it here. I try to keep myself busy to make the time pass, but the slowness of the day makes it drag. I have to fight all of the urges inside me to lock up early and get on the road to Florida, to Lori. But, I can't do it. I learned a long time ago that if the hours on the door say you are going to be open till 6:00 p.m., then you had better make sure that you are there till 6:00 p.m. I don't know if we will sell anything if I stay, but I know for sure I will not sell anything if I leave.

A young woman, really just a girl not much out of high school, comes. She looks strangely familiar, but I don't know from where. Maybe one of the checkers at the grocery store. I smile and nod at her as I say, "Last-minute Christmas shopping?"

"No," she answers shyly, looking down at the floor. "You don't remember me, do you?"

When she speaks, I remember her. She was the girl who was with the Mexican when I first met him. "Oh, yeah, I do remember you." She was dressed normally this time, in just a touch of tasteful makeup and University of Missouri black and gold sweats. "How are you?" What I really wanted to know was what she wanted.

"I'm good," she said, again shyly while looking everywhere around the room except directly at me. "I just wanted to, um, I just wanted to, I guess, I mean to say, well, thanks."

"I'm not sure what you're thanking me for."

153

"You stood up to Emilio. You didn't do what he wanted you to do. That was more courageous than you probably think. He was very angry."

I pause watching her closely, trying to read her body language. What is she setting me up for? I look to see who is parked outside. What's going on? The only car on the lot is an empty, older model Toyota. She picks up on my apprehension. "It's just me, no one is with me," she says. Slightly smiling, her cute young face exposes at least one missing tooth, which she fights the smile back to hide.

"Was he your boyfriend or what?"

Smirking, she says, "Boyfriend? Really? Did he look like my boyfriend when we were here together?"

"I didn't mean anything by it. I guess I'm just curious what you want from me."

"Nothing. I thank you for standing up to him because that is what got him killed. You see, as long as Emilio was alive, I was not free. Emilio owned me. So I want to thank you for that."

"Owned you?"

"My stepmother, who raised me, lives in New Mexico. She owed him money for drugs. She is a good woman, really, but she has a terrible problem with drugs." She looks down to the floor again trying to hide the tears welled up in her dark brown eyes. "He was going to kill her, so I offered myself to him as payment of the debt. So, he owned me."

"I don't know what to say."

Interstate Motorcycles

"You don't need to say anything," she says as she looks up, unable to hold back either the smile or the streaks of tears on her cheeks. "No one ever disobeyed him, and lived. So, thank you! He would eventually have killed me too. The only way I could be set free from him was for one of us to end up dead. Thank you for being the cause that it turned out to be Emilio dead, and not me. That's what I wanted to thank you for."

"You don't have to thank me for anything. I didn't do anything courageous, just stupid I think. So what do you do now?"

"I'm driving back to New Mexico to find my stepmom. When I left with Emilio, we never thought we would see each other again."

"You're driving to New Mexico in that?" I ask, pointing at the old Toyota.

"It's not so bad. Emilio and I drove up here in it when we left Tulsa. I've got a little cash, should be enough for gas. I'll make it."

"Why don't you sell it and buy a bus ticket?"

"I probably couldn't get much for it. Besides, who would buy it?"

"I'll give you five hundred dollars for it."

"Five hundred dollars?"

"Yeah, here you go," I say, handing her the very same cash that Muntze gave to me.

"What?"

"Yeah, I'll take it off your hands."

She looks at the money, then at me, and asks, "Why do you want it?"

"Two reasons. First, I can sell it for parts and be ahead a few bucks. Second, I don't think that thing will make it all the back to New Mexico. We both come out ahead if you sell it to me."

"Well, all right. I'll sell it."

Right then the boarded-up front door opens and in strolls Tim Walker. "I love what you've done with the place," he says and laughs, looking around at the plywood-covered glass. "You want to come over and remodel my place too?"

"How are you, Tim? I didn't think I would be seeing you around for a while." Emilio's girl withdrew toward the customer waiting area as Tim approached.

"Well, I'm still looking to get some tires on the old Harley."

"You can bring it in any time. We will take care of you. I owe you, dude. I appreciate you putting me together with Muntze."

"I'm glad he could help you," Tim says.

"So, how do you know him?"

"I was in prison with his brother, Jim. He's a lot like Greg, except he caught twelve years for manslaughter when he got out of the army. He beat his ex-wife's new boyfriend to death

Interstate Motorcycles

for slapping her around. He told me that some people just have a good killing coming."

"Hmm, that sounds familiar," I tell him.

"So, who's that?" Tim asks in a low voice as he looks toward the waiting area. "She looks familiar."

"She was with El Elegido. She says that one of them owned her. She is trying to get back to New Mexico. I told her I would drop her off at the bus station."

"I thought that was her. I seen her at the bar. She cleans up pretty good, huh? I'll drop her off at the Greyhound then grab the bike and bring it back to here, if she doesn't mind."

She didn't, and as they leave together the phone rings for what might be the first time all day. "Is this Mike?" a familiar-sounding voice that I don't actually recognize asks.

"Yeah, this is Mike. What can I fix you up with?"

"Mike, It's Kat, Kat Stevens, the trucker that you let stay with you a couple of weeks ago. What's been going on?"

"Not much," he wouldn't believe the truth if I told him. "How's the new job?"

"It's great! They run only new trucks in excellent condition and I've got an easy, regular run up and down the west coast every week. I actually get all of my weekends off. I'm finally going to have time now to find that permanent church I told you I wished for, and I'll be able to do more motorcycle riding. What a great Christmas gift, huh? Hey, I was wondering, do you still have that Guzzi, the California Vintage?"

"Yeah, I still have it, but I've got a couple of guys hovering around it. It might be sold any day now."

"Fifteen thousand, right? Well, Mike, um, if no one has a deposit on it yet, um . . . I think I'll take it."

I know darn good and well he doesn't have that kind of money. "What?"

"I'm not kidding. I want the bike."

"We are talking fifteen thousand—*dollars*—right?"

Kat laughs. "Yes, fifteen thousand dollars. I know I told you I didn't have the money, but actually I do now, and I would really like to buy that motorcycle from you. I got a severance settlement from my old company and a signing bonus with the new outfit who I am thrilled to be with and planning to stay. There has been a vintage motorcycle collector in Connecticut who has been interested in my old Police Special for a couple of years, so I called him and sold it. All of that together leaves me with more than enough cash right now to buy it from you and I really want it. I've been thinking about it ever since you showed it to me."

Still a little speechless, I say, "Well, uh, that's . . . great."

"I could either send you a check or, if you would rather, I can get my bank to electronically transfer it to you today. Then, if you don't mind, I'll make arrangements to get the bike picked up early next year."

"The transfer would be great. I will tag the bike sold and keep it for you here as long as you need."

"Thanks, Mike! Merry Christmas."

Interstate Motorcycles

He wasn't kidding. I gave him the bank routing and account numbers he needed and we had the money in the bank by closing time. The sale netted us enough to get all of our due invoices settled through the end of the year, plus a few bucks for the trip to Pensacola.

April 5, 2010

"Lori! Oh, Lori," I bellow from the garage as I complete the pre-ride inspection of the idling V1100 Breva, readying it and myself for the ride to work. It is going to be a busy day.

"What?" she answers incredulously as she throws back the door between our kitchen and the garage. "What are you yelling about?"

Look at her! She gets more beautiful with every passing day. I just admire her for a moment, taking in this gorgeous woman who shares my life. How lucky am I! "I just wanted to tell you that I love you."

Her demeanor changes from defensive to happy. "I love you too. I'll see you at work in a couple of hours. I have to wash my hair this morning, you know?"

"You look fine."

Interstate Motorcycles

She fluffs her hair, winks, and goes back inside as I mount the bike and click it into gear. Easing out of the driveway, admiring all of the tender new leaves the early spring has brought out of the trees, I intentionally turn in the direction opposite the way to work to take the long way in.

As I accelerate smoothly up the hill, I feel that old familiar anticipation. Remarkably, after all of these years, I still feel that high school kid excitement. It's not all that different now than it was the very first time I rode a motorcycle. It's that splendid blend of exhilaration and relaxation that comes while rolling the throttle on and shifting through the gears, pointing the bike in the direction of some of my favorite turns and letting the motorcycle do what it does best.

Motorcycles are turning instruments. They are constructed front to back and top to bottom with the mission of applying its horsepower to the pavement effectively, carrying its payload smoothly and accurately. Not simply in straight lines, but more importantly through turns. No matter where you're riding and where you are going, you are going to turn. A motorcycle rider cannot simply rotate a wheel into and out of the direction desired like an automobile. Turning a motorcycle requires more activity on the part of the operator, more cooperation. The rider and the machine must work together. The rider has to diagnose the intensity of the turn angle, its available traction, and potential traffic and geographic hazards while approaching it, and adjust speed accordingly. Too slow and the motorcycle wobbles and wanders around the turn, trying to find a proper way through. Too fast for the machine and its operator's ability, and they both run wide, sometimes resulting in catastrophe. Once the correct speed is achieved based on thorough observation, the angle of attack has to be properly and smoothly obtained. The rider has to lean his or her whole weight toward the turn with the motorcycle. The handlebars must be ever so gently adjusted left and right to rotate the motorcycle in toward the turn's apex and then back out again. The engine's speed and the load on the bike's suspension components play their part in the concert. If a passenger is aboard with the operator, the passenger must also join the activity. Every part and aspect comes to bear on the turning, or riding a motorcycle becomes an endeavor somewhere between confusing and purely dangerous. An experienced rider in command of a finely tuned motorcycle is a beautiful and graceful event. A ballet performed sans an orchestra and at super highway speeds.

The long way to work is a ten-mile rural two-laner with over fifty turns, each one like an old friend to me after all of the times I've taken it. Left—and right-handers, some are long sweepers and others tight hairpins. Hills and valleys are part of the experience as well, with each elevation change adding to the challenge of proper and brisk execution.

The last couple months have gone fast. I wish it was because we had more business than we could handle, but that's not why. We have been busy rebuilding the damaged showroom, coordinating between our insurance company and contractors. The job is finished now and the results are impressive. All new glass on the building and a new all-glass, double-wide front door. The interior walls have been repaired and painted. No trace of the many bullet holes exists. All of the damage to the motorcycles has been repaired and the damaged merchandise has been replaced. Muntze was right. The place does look better than ever.

The ride seems too short, as though I just began the backyard adventure and it's already over. The shop is in sight and I'm on final approach. I bend the bike to the right, hot into the last turn taking me off of the road and onto the shop's parking lot gently lifting the rear wheel in a *stoppie* precisely at the new front door. Adam comes out. He has gotten here ahead

Interstate Motorcycles

of me. Right behind him is Deputy Tom Hughes, holding a folder.

"Hi, Tom, Adam. What's up?"

"Mike," Tom begins quickly while looking into the folder. "I need to talk to you for a second."

Great! What now? "Sure Tom, how can I help you?"

"Well," he says, clearing his throat, "it seems I have a warrant for your arrest."

I'm beginning to think that I may never have this incident behind me, and now a warrant? "You have a warrant for me, for what?" I ask him feeling the adrenaline level rise.

"Well, Mike, it seems you got a speeding ticket last December. It looks here like you never appeared to pay the fine. Could you get to the court house today and take care of that so I don't have to lock you up?"

"I promise," I answer, sighing.

Tom cuts me a salute and heads to his cruiser saying, "Don't forget. Oh, and slow down, will you?"

"Okay, okay, I will. Good grief."

"And you were having such a nice day," Adam says, stepping forward. "You must have come to work the long way?" He knows me.

"As a matter of fact, I did."

The early spring weather has reignited business. We are jammed in the service department. Not only is Adam working overtime, but we have hired two new technicians. "Well, here's what we've got today..." He's a great kid. While I'm still getting my helmet, gloves, and jacket off, he gives me a report and shop schedule for the day ahead of us. As always, the plan is perfect. "How's that sound?"

"Great! Let's go to work."

We have been busy on the sales floor as well, with many new faces coming in to shop for just the right new motorcycle. Our sales numbers are still not up to 2006 and 2007 levels, but they are improving. I'll take it. Parts and accessory sales are on par for a decent year as well. All in all, I'm encouraged. We still have a long way to go to dig out of the hole we have fallen into through the last couple of years and the recession's effect on us, but we will keep on working on it. What else can I do but keep working on it? I think I was born an entrepreneur. It's in my DNA. As a teenager, I became a motorcyclist. As a young adult, I married the love of my life, and then all of the ingredients were in place to become a motorcycle dealer. So I did. It never has been, nor will be, an easy job. It is ever changing and constantly more challenging. I will never get famous for it. The town square will never have a statue of me, and I will never strike it rich. But if I put in long hours and work hard, I can make a decent living, and I wouldn't trade it for any other way of life.

I have lived the unique experience of selecting something I have a passion for doing and turning it into a career. I have lived with the ability to wake up every morning, chart my own course, trim my own rigging, and set sail on life's sea. Some years the sea and winds have been fair and favorable. Other years have been stormy and treacherous, and we have been blown off course and run aground in places that we did not know and did not want to be. It could have cost me the business. It could

Interstate Motorcycles

even have cost me my life. But at the end of the day, whether success or failure, rise or fall, for better or worse, whatever the outcome, I can own it. There's no one else to credit, and there's no one else to blame. Exhilarating and free, like motorcycling itself. Will the store succeed going forward? I don't know, but we're doing all right today, and that's enough. I've learned that in the end I want to look back over a lifetime and be thankful to God, not necessarily for the outcome but for the opportunities I've had.

In the last four or five months, I have learned a few other things about the Almighty, things that were in me since my childhood. Things that my father wanted me to know, even when he was struggling. I've learned that *God is*. During those times when he seemed distant, or even nonexistent, God hadn't moved—I had. I've learned that God doesn't want a lot of religious activity from me; he wants me. I've learned that my negative assessment of churches for religious behavior I can't agree with is just as wrong as churches negatively assessing me for rejecting human-inspired religious traditions. I've learned that church attendance isn't about what kind of people are sitting around me, but it is about whose house we are all sitting in. I've learned that connecting with God isn't as difficult as we make it. Jesus was born a man and preached a covenant between God and man that is as simple and straight forward as it gets. Believe in God, and believe that Jesus is who he said he was. Don't try to rationalize it or figure out how it works. Just believe it. *"For God so loved the world . . . that whoever believes in him shall not perish"* (John 3:16 NIV). *"Whoever believes in him is not condemned"* (John 3:18 NIV).

Jesus boiled it down into two succinct instructions. When a religious teacher of that time asked him which is the greatest commandment in the law, he replied, *"Love the Lord your God with all your heart and with all your soul and with all your mind. This is the first and greatest commandment. And the second is like it: Love your neighbor as yourself. All the law and the prophets hang on these two commands"* (Matthew 22: 34–40 NIV). He wasn't referring to a warm, fuzzy, emotional love. Those feelings are fleeting and often disappear like a vapor. Everyone loves that new motorcycle, until the first payment is due. He was referring to love the *action*. Love the verb. Love must be something that we do by an act of the will and not just because it makes us feel good. Love is what perseveres when it stops feeling good, when it hurts, or when it could even be dangerous. The kind of love Lori and I have for each other cements us together in good times and in bad. I experienced that love in the actions of people through my experience with El Elegido. Tim Walker put himself in harm's way simply out of a heartfelt concern for my safety. There was nothing in it for him to introduce me to Greg Muntze, and getting involved could have gotten him shot too. Greg Muntze put himself in even greater danger, not only out of a concern that the guys he was tracking were dangerous and that I and others were going to be killed if they weren't stopped, but also out of a love he felt for a liquor store owner's family in Tulsa who he got to too late to save. I experienced the great love of a young woman who sold herself into the hands of a murdering weapons trafficker to save her stepmother's life. And she thought something I did was courageous? Even the stumbling and bumbling Bob Culp, in what ultimately turned out to be his final act, demonstrated love for me beyond measure, taking the extra time to warn me about the danger I was in. I don't know it for certain, but that extra time he took before getting on the run may have been what cost him his life.

Those are examples of love I found in my world, not hidden in a church. Tangible examples of love I experienced as answered prayers even though I was making bad decisions and moving farther away from what I knew was right. Those are examples of the persistent, relentless love God has for us. He loves us in the verb form. Not because we deserve it, but

Interstate Motorcycles

because *he is*, and he does. All he wants from us in return is to believe it and love him back, in the verb form.

That's the love that has me back in church on Sunday mornings alongside Lori. There are still people who I disagree with, but I don't focus on any of that now; it's all meaningless. I'm there working on loving the Lord more and loving those I disagree with despite our different perspectives. I just want to be there, present and accounted for, up front in the center section, right up to the end.

Just like my dad.

ABOUT THE AUTHOR

BILL DUNKUS IS A lifelong motorcycle enthusiast and dealer, husband, father, grandfather, and follower of Christ. While enthusiastically pursuing motorcycling, he had the opportunity to spend fifteen years running the motorcycle repair division for the St. Louis Metropolitan Police Department, where he began writing for a number of publications, including a regular column in *The Gendarme*, the official publication of the St. Louis Police Officers Association, and regular columns and features for both *The Civilian News* and *The Police News*. Since then, he has been a freelance writer for a number of motorcycling publications, offering not only stories based on years of experience but technical writings and service bulletins. Bill Dunkus continues to pursue motorcycling and can be found many weekends on a road course somewhere riding in Formula 40 (riders forty years old and up) Champion Cup Series road races. On weekdays he is at his own small motorcycle dealership in Rolla, Missouri. El Elegido is based loosely on actual people and events he has known and experienced. Any time his hands aren't on a motorcycle, they are probably pounding away on the keyboard of his laptop, crafting another story.